To
Avril

I have a fun read

+ +

name

THE INCEPTOR TRILOGY
VOLUME 2
THE PATIENT

Maureen Farenden

Book Guild Publishing
Sussex, England

First published in Great Britain in 2007 by
The Book Guild Ltd
Pavilion View
19 New Road
Brighton, BN1 1UF

Typesetting in Baskerville by
Keyboard Services, Luton, Bedfordshire

Printed in Great Britain by
CPI Bath

A catalogue record for this book is available from
The British Library

ISBN 978 1 84624 099 7

Contents

1

The Old Woman

While Charity visits Sam in hospital there's another patient, an old woman, in the corner of the ward who's constantly calling to her while struggling with the breathing mask on her face. 'Miss, Miss, come here, come here; hurry, my dear, before they come back.'

'Why do you keep looking over into the corner, there's nothing there?' Sam asks, annoyed at not receiving her full attention, while munching away at the chocolates and grapes Charity brought her.

'Can't you hear her? The old woman in the bed keeps calling to me.' Charity replies, surprised that no one else in the ward is taking any notice of the noisy patient in the corner.

'What old woman? There's no one there! The bed's been empty since I came in this morning,' retorts Sam as she stares inquiringly over at the empty bed.

Immediately Charity senses that 'other forces' are calling to her. 'I won't be long, Sam, I'm just going to see what she wants.'

'Here we go again! I pop into hospital for a couple of days for a minor op' and end up sharing a ward with a ghost. I suppose I shouldn't be surprised, after all not everyone has a best friend who happens to be a world renowned psychic investigator,' grumbles Sam as she stuffs another chocolate in her mouth.

Charity walks over to the old woman, who looks very frail and surrounded by machines and tubes with a mask over her face enabling her to breathe.

'Oh thank you, my dear, come closer, come closer, for I don't want them to hear,' she whispers, almost unable to breathe as she pulls the mask off revealing deep blue tragic eyes sunken into a very old lined face that's pale and edged with sadness.

'What is it that you seek?' Charity asks as her gift of 'Clear Seeing' is already telling her that this is only the beginning...

The old woman indicates for Charity to bend over as she whispers in her ear: 'They want what I know, but I was too clever for them and made myself invisible. Everyone knows me, but no one knows me, as I'm invisible. I was too clever for them and they'll never find it now. I win, I win, they lose, they lose. How clever I've been, my dear, but you know, don't you, don't you.' Her voice grows weaker and weaker until finally, just before she breathes her last breath of life, she looks deep into Charity's eyes and smiles, saying 'Thank you, my dear, thank you.'

Just at that moment the ward sister passes as Charity asks, 'There was an old woman in this bed that died recently. Can you tell me who she was?'

'You mean Blank Liz,' she replies, looking puzzled that anybody would be interested in her.

'That's a strange name. Why was she called that?'

'She didn't have a name. She lived rough on the streets and was always in and out of here over the years, and whenever anyone asked her name she'd just reply, "I'm invisible, I have no name, I'm blank". So we nick-named her Blank Liz, which seemed to please her and always made her giggle.' The nurse paused for a second then added, 'It's almost as if she was proud of being

2

known as "blank". Sadly the last time she came in we couldn't help her and she died yesterday at eleven. No one's come to claim her body so I suppose the State will bury her with the name "Blank Liz" on her gravestone.'

The sister rushes off to attend to another patient leaving Charity staring at the empty bed as she remembers the old woman's last words: 'Thank you, my dear, thank you', before returning to Sam, who by now is so fed up she's eaten the whole box of chocolates and nearly all the grapes as well.

'Well, what did you find out?' she snaps, irritated at being ignored for so long.

'Apparently there was an old lady in the bed who died yesterday and according to the ward sister she lived rough on the streets and appeared to have no name so they nicknamed her Blank Liz.'

'Blank Liz! What kind of name's that? What a sad life she must've had to die with no name,' she replies suddenly feeling rather selfish after hearing Charity's sad tale.

'I know, Sam, but she did have a name and was somebody and didn't live a Blank life, but chose her life for a reason. Why would someone choose to give up their name and their life? I'm going to find out who she was and why she chose to be "invisible". She called to me for a reason. She wants her life and her name back! She wants her real name put on her gravestone and she's charged me with that quest.'

Sam smiles quietly to herself while finishing her last grape; for she knows her dear friend so well and when the spirits call to her for help she can't refuse them.

'Well I guess this means the RING's on another case and I haven't even had time to enjoy being sick yet,' chuckles Sam as the two of them look at each other, little realising that they are about to embark on what will become an epic journey into the past, which will uncover betrayal, deceit, envy, greed, hatred, lies, lost love, lust and murder.

2

Angel of Judgement

'Right, put your dressing-gown on as we're off to the morgue to check out the body of our client before it gets taken away,' Charity announces, pulling the bedclothes off Sam as she grabs her dressing-gown from the locker next to the bed.

'What! Hang on a second here, I'm hardly in a position to go traipsing around the hospital looking for dead bodies and I certainly have no intention of visiting another morgue especially after what happened last time with our American spirit, and I have no desire to be locked in a freezer again thank you very much. Besides, look at me, I look terrible, my hair's a mess, I've no make-up on and I'm sick! I've just recovered from a major operation and was expecting some sympathy and gentle loving care from my oldest and dearest friend.' Sam is so vain that the idea of walking around the hospital and bumping into someone she knows is too horrifying a prospect to contemplate.

'Oh, Sam, you do make me laugh. Major operation indeed! An ingrowing toenail can hardly be classed as "major", besides, what's the alternative, sit here bored out of your mind for the next couple of days or come on an adventure with me? Now you know you're just as interested in finding out about our spirit as I am.' Charity

5

chuckles to herself as she watches Sam checking herself out in the mirror, hastily applying her essential beauty items that she'll take to the grave with her: red lipstick, eyeliner and powder. She combs and sprays her spiky black hair to complete the illusion of natural glamour.

'Have I got time to change? Dressing-gowns aren't exactly the most flattering of outfits,' grumbles Sam as she checks out her silhouette in the slim mirror hanging on the back her locker door. 'Oh bum! You do land me in it sometimes, old girl.'

'No,' replies Charity quickly as she grabs her arm and drags her through the ward into the corridor. 'We haven't much time; anyway spirits aren't interested in what you're wearing, besides, you can look great in five minutes whereas it takes me at least forty-five.'

'Oh is that so?' says Sam chirpily, now that her ego has been stroked.

The bell rings and the lift doors spring back as they both tentatively step out into the dark corridor leading to the morgue, looking all around just in case. For though Charity shows no fear to Sam, she still remembers their near fatal encounter with the 'Dark One' the last time they were in a morgue visiting her client Stephen Mallon, the American spirit. Even though they won that battle against her arch enemy, Lucifer, she's all too aware that the war between good and evil continues and that he can summon the evil demons and spirits of the dark at any time and anywhere in his constant quest to eliminate her and take control of the mortal world. Therefore wherever she is and whoever she's with vigilance is her constant companion, coupled with the knowledge that she has the protection of God's divine intervention. So with her army of angels, the spirits of the light and her beloved Ma and Pa (now happily reunited in the spirit world) to watch over her and her loved ones she continues her vocation as the Inceptor, helping those in both the spirit and mortal world in their search for justice, peace, redemption and truth.

As they make their way along the dark corridor to the light at the end, their eyes dart everywhere. Sam keeps looking behind her, for if there's one thing she hates, it's being in dark places that are eerily quiet except for the sound of her own footsteps. Finally they make it to the doorway leading into the morgue only to discover that it's locked and entry is by way of a security intercom system.

'What'll we do now? Whoever's in charge isn't just going to let us in without good reason. I mean we hardly look kosher with me in my dressing-gown and you looking highly suspicious,' Sam mumbles as she nervously looks around the corridor expecting dark demons and spirits to materialise at any minute.

'Just a minute, how come I look suspicious and you don't?' Charity retorts as they stand back to back so that every part of the corridor is within their view. They hear a familiar sound echoing out from the intercom, which warms their hearts and suddenly things don't seem so bad. They giggle like a couple of school girls at the million to one chance of hearing this particular voice again.

'Turn around (sniff, sniff) and face the camera please (sniff, sniff); only authorised personnel are allowed down here (sniff, sniff).'

As they hear the last sniff, sniff, they both turn and grin into the camera.

'I don't believe it (sniff, sniff), it can't be (sniff, sniff)? Is it really you, Miss Holmes and Miss Francis (sniff, sniff).'

'It is indeed, Andy, my old chum, and what a pleasant surprise to hear your dulcet tones again even if it is in another morgue.'

7

The intercom buzzes and the door opens and once again a familiar feeling of déjà vu comes over them as the three stand in silence momentarily remembering what happened the last time they were all together at the village of Kradlived in the pagan church of Noddegamra where the Final Reckoning took place. A time they all hope and pray will never ever come again.

'It's so good to see you again, Miss Holmes (sniff, sniff), although I've a feeling this isn't a social call and that you're on one of your quests again (sniff, sniff). Please tell me that it's not another Armageddon (sniff, sniff), for I've only just started this job and there aren't that many mortuaries I can keep moving to (sniff, sniff).'

'It's so good to see you too, Andy, but what are you doing here?' Charity asks, hugging him, for she truly is pleased to see him; that nervous little man who stood up to the 'Dark Trio' and fought so bravely with her at the Final Reckoning and for whom her admiration is limitless.

'Oh I just couldn't continue working at the morgue after what happened there, Miss Holmes (sniff, sniff), it seemed possessed somehow (sniff, sniff). I swear there were times when I could feel the "Dark Trio" shadowing me (sniff, sniff) and the place began to have a dark feel about it (sniff, sniff). Eventually one morning I couldn't go into work (sniff, sniff) and that was it. I moved jobs (sniff, sniff) and found this position and I'm really happy here, Miss Holmes (sniff, sniff), so please don't summon any more evil spirits (sniff, sniff) because I really don't think I could go through it again (sniff, sniff).'

'I'm really sorry you had to move jobs, Andy, but you, of all people, should know that our destinies are already foretold and meeting you here today just confirms that.' Charity smiles gently at him, but underneath, her gift of

8

'Clear Seeing' is telling her that perhaps her guardian angels led Andy here to help her again.

'Oh I never thought of it like that, Miss Holmes (sniff, sniff). So you really think our paths were meant to cross again (sniff, sniff)?' asks Andy, suddenly feeling very important again, but still terrified at what favour Charity is about to ask of him and what the consequences are going to be for him if he helps her.

'Oh absolutely, Andy, no doubt about it, destiny has crossed our paths again and we must respond otherwise the future is lost,' replies Charity in that cryptic tone that she uses when drawing people into her thoughts so that she can help those lost spirits from the 'Middle Life' who've called to her for help; in this case the old woman. While Andy continues to sniff nervously and Sam helps herself to some coffee in his office, Charity already senses that there's a presence in the room and silently performs the chakras (seven energies within her body positioned along the line of the spine) to open up her mind to the Universal Unconscious, which enables her to enter the world of spirits and communicate to them through her 'all-seeing third eye', also known as 'Clear Seeing'. Slowly she hears the faint voice of the old woman calling to her.

'I'm here, my dear, come quickly before they take me. Hurry please, hurry, my dear, don't let them take me, please hurry, my dear.'

Charity closes her eyes to concentrate her all-seeing third eye to picture where she is.

'Are you OK? You're beginning to scare me. I don't want to be locked in any more freezers,' cries Sam as she notices Charity going into one of her trances and feels the room becoming much colder, while Andy starts sniffing and breathing faster and faster as he realises that he's in for another visitation from the spirit world.

Suddenly the locks on one of the refrigeration units unclip and the slab inside containing a body covered in a white sheet leaps out. At the same time the room begins to close in as the world of spirits starts to enter the mortal world through the doorway that's been opened up by Charity in the deepest parts of her mind by performing the chakras.

'Oh no, here we go again. How come I always get caught in the morgue when there's spirits around and I'm not even dressed? What a way to go! Done in by a spirit in my dressing-gown; sometimes being your best friend is just too much,' shrieks Sam as she drops her coffee and rushes towards Charity and Andy, who's clinging on tightly to his desk. Charity slowly opens her eyes to see Sam and Andy practically glued to her out of fear as all three look over at the body lying under the sheet, which is floating just above the slab surrounded by a brilliant light.

'Oh no, oh no (sniff, sniff), please tell me these are good spirits, Miss Holmes (sniff, sniff),' laments Andy as he prays silently.

'I'm with Andy on this one,' chips in Sam, clinging on tightly to Charity's arm as they watch the white sheet fall from the floating body to reveal the old woman. From within the light a winged angel appears holding the horn of judgement, which, when he blows it, brings forth the resurrection of past souls to judge and pass sentence upon you (in this instance the old woman). He's a dazzling angel of refulgence and splendour dressed in flowing emerald green and gold robes with golden hair and magnificent blood red wings, which when spread high above him, cover the entire room in darkness and under which he cradles the past souls that have risen from their watery graves. He's the **Angel of Judgement**, sent by God to judge the old woman in the 'Court of

Past Souls' (past mortals whose life and death have been affected by her actions during her lifetime and who now have the chance to claim justice for any wrong that she's committed towards them and finally receive redemption for their sins). The decision of this court is final and irreversible so therefore every opportunity is afforded to the old woman to plead her case. Each past soul comes forward to show a glimpse of her life and how it affected theirs until all the evidence has been presented and only then will the **Angel of Judgement** make his decision that'll seal her fate, which can be one of three. She can enter the Middle Life, where souls await entry into heaven once redemption is theirs, which can be for all eternity and where they'll never feel the pleasures of heaven if the past can't be undone and forgiveness given (these are the tortured souls that often visit Charity in her psychic dreams pleading for help and redemption). She can enter the afterlife (heaven), where she can join her loved ones and know the unquantifiable pleasure of complete love and peace. Or finally she can enter the 'Dark Life' (hell) where only an eternity of misery and pain awaits her.

Suddenly the room is filled with a dark thunderous sound that almost shatters their ear drums, which as it echoes through every corner of the morgue causes mirrors, cups, office and technical equipment to shatter and break. It's the horn of judgement bringing forth the past souls from underneath the **Angel of Judgement**'s magnificent wings as they appear one by one to stand in front of the old woman, whose body is now standing upright floating above the mortuary slab facing the Court of Past Souls. Her eyes open slowly to reveal the same sad, tragic look that Charity saw when she removed the mask. She faces her court of accusers and defenders who'll decide her final fate.

The **Angel of Judgement** looks down upon the old woman and asks in a strong detached voice that echoes around the mortuary, 'Is there anyone here who'll defend you against your accusers?'

The old woman looks up at the angel then down at the line of past souls in front of her before turning and looking over at Charity, who along with Sam and Andy can see the anguish and despair in her face. She stares directly at Charity for what seems an eternity without saying a single word. None is needed as Charity looks deep into her tortured face and sees that this isn't an evil woman, but a frightened and betrayed woman whose battle for dignity and hope led her into a dark world, which she was ill-equipped to fight in yet had no choice if she was to survive. A woman whose heart and soul is good, but in order to stay alive had to become like her enemies, and in doing so lost her own identity. A woman whose only wish now is to retrieve her name and move on into the afterlife with the dignity and pride that was not afforded to her during her mortal life. This is a woman who never had the hand of true friendship bestowed upon her or experienced the purity of true love freely given to her and therefore stole what she felt would give her the life that she so desperately desired and that fate had so cruelly denied her. A woman who had the ability of greatness within her but was forced to become invisible. A truly amazing woman born into the wrong world at the wrong time and who's already paid a high price for her sins. No, this is a woman who, although she has lied and cheated and felt envy and hatred towards others in her life, has also had great injustices perpetrated against her and is deserving of a second chance at happiness. This is a woman that Charity knows she must defend otherwise her vocation as an Inceptor will be meaningless.

'I'll defend her,' Charity shouts in a fearless voice, which startles Sam and Andy as they look at her with pride and admiration at accepting the awesome task before her. The old woman closes her eyes for a moment, breathing in the air of hope as finally the hand of true friendship has been imparted to her and she's no longer alone in her battle to reclaim not only her name but also her dignity and everlasting peace in the afterlife. Slowly she opens them and once again looks over at Charity smiling and for the first time her face glows with an inner happiness that she'd never felt when mortal. She repeats the words, 'Thank you, my dear, thank you.'

The horn of judgement sounds again as the **Angel of Judgement** pronounces the court open and the past comes forward to claim its prize: the old woman's soul.

3

Court of Past Souls

Three ghostly white translucent souls come forth from under the **Angel of Judgement**'s wings: a husband and wife and their daughter (a twin) to stand before the old woman. The husband steps forward two paces until he's directly beneath her. As Charity looks closer into his inner soul she sees an elderly man aged about 70 with a slight, almost emaciated frame, that she senses was once tall and upright. His receding white hair is parted in the middle, combed and greased flat onto his head, while his white moustache is cut and trimmed tight over his thin lips. This was once a proud and honourable man who enjoyed status and respect in his mortal life, but fell from grace and is now doomed to wander in the Middle Life until he repents for his sins and redemption is granted. He looks directly at the old woman, raising his arm in the air, pointing his finger accusingly as he says loudly, 'You took what wasn't yours and I paid the price for your sin, you wicked girl, and now it's your turn to pay and release me from this purgatory that has been my penance for the last forty-five years. Retribution will be mine.'

Silence surrounds the room as the bitterness in his voice cuts through the air, while Charity, Sam and Andy look at each other wondering what sin this old woman could have committed that would destroy this man's life.

'How do you answer your accuser?' The **Angel of Judgement** looks down upon the old woman, while she suddenly gains strength in her voice, speaking out defiantly.

'You stole my life through your silence and you dare to seek retribution. Look into your own soul and tell the truth; only then will you be free. I did what I had to do but you knew the truth and said nothing. I'm not the guilty one here and you know that to be true.'

The old woman turns to Charity, pleading. 'You can see the truth in this man's soul. Am I not allowed any justice even in death? Help me, my dear, for I'm too tired and too old to fight this court on my own.'

Charity moves towards the vision to look deeper into the old woman's eyes and sees that the pain is real and knows instantly that her accuser has indeed done an injustice towards her. She then turns to face the old man, asking, 'What was taken and what is the truth that you dare not tell?'

He looks down towards the floor for the shame he feels is real and yet he's still unable to speak the truth even though it would release his tortured soul. Slowly he raises his head until he's face to face with the old woman. They stare at each other intensely before he turns towards Charity, saying, 'I'm unable to answer either of your questions, but I will give you a date: **21st June 1940**. Go back to this date and search for the truth and then you'll know what was taken and who the guilty one in this court is.'

Slowly he steps back into the line of his fellow accusers as his wife steps forward two paces until she too is standing directly beneath the old woman. They both glare at each other. Her demeanour is that of a proud and arrogant woman. She must be about 75 and has a sharp bitter face that shows no compassion for the old woman whose destiny is in her hands. She's taller and more upright than her husband, with long white hair that's scraped back off her face and tied up in a tight bun. This makes her look harsh and unforgiving. She has no grace and instead wallows in anger and hatred, which has kept her soul bound to her husband's in the Middle Life, where they both are unable to give each other the comfort that should be afforded to a loving couple.

Charity senses that the hatred emitting from these two elderly women is so strong that it almost destroys any feeling of warmth and pity she feels for them. Whatever happened between these two all those decades ago, it's still so powerful that even in death it can't be broken, and yet Charity senses that this hatred is born out of love; a pure love that transcends all others and yet the recipient of this love is neither deserving or grateful. A love that's caused so much pain and sorrow that it's crossed over into the spirit world and is still as malevolent today as it was all those lost years ago. She spits out her words injuriously towards the old woman as they float through the air like poisonous venom.

'We took you into our home and gave you food and shelter and you repaid us with lies and deceit. You lusted after what wasn't yours and when you couldn't have it you stole, leaving us with nothing. Now finally you'll pay for what you did to our family and my revenge will be to watch you suffer for all eternity.'

The old women stare at each other bitterly as the accusing words linger in the air before the **Angel of Judgement** again asks. 'How do you answer your accuser?'

'You gave me nothing,' the old woman replies angrily as she forms a fist and strikes her arm in the air with such a force that her accuser steps back in horror. 'I was an innocent with an open heart and a giving soul and you destroyed all of that, leaving me an empty shell with no name and no future. I came into your home full of

16

hope and aspirations only to discover a world of envy, greed and betrayal. I left behind a poor but loving world and entered the darkness of loneliness and despair where you stole my dreams of a better life. Now you dare to challenge me in this court. Well I'm not in your world now and you shall speak the truth and give me back my name.'

The old woman turns again to Charity, only this time she's not pleading for help but asking for understanding and a second chance.

'I did wrong. This I don't deny, but I learned from the experts and had no choice. Ask her now to speak the truth and end this torment that's been my burden for so long. Let not pride be our downfall, but better still forgiveness be our rebirth.'

Charity moves closer until she's able to push her hand through the translucent body of the accusing wife (as Sam and Andy look on in amazement) to enable her to use her powerful psychic powers to connect with this angry and tortured soul and see the real truth within her. As she closes her eyes she's transported back in time to a world of war where Britain is in its darkest hours. It's 1940 and there's water, British warships and men in dark suits talking in secret behind closed doors as other men in pinstriped suits are rushing to work in the grey streets of the City where powerful forces are at work. Suddenly the vision travels across the Atlantic and Charity sees another City, Montreal in Canada, where deep underground there lies a secret between these two powerful countries. Suddenly Charity feels a sharp pain racing through her hand as if she's been stabbed by a dagger, and pulls back as the vision disappears.

'You've seen enough,' are the cruel words spoken by the wife as she steps back to stand by her husband. Now the third soul steps forward. She too is an old woman who died at the age of 72, yet Charity's gift tells her that she's their daughter. In the world of spirits if you die with darkness and sin on your soul you remain as you are and don't revert to the youthfulness and beauty of your prime. She died an old woman as did her parents before her and all three have remained that way for they've yet to repent and feel God's divine hand of forgiveness upon them. Until their souls let go of all the hate within them they'll remain tortured spirits unable to pass onto the afterlife. As she moves closer towards the old woman she trembles with rage, raising both arms in the air even though her body is ravaged with the pain of old age. She's much smaller than her mother but has the same pride and arrogance about her, with cold dark eyes and fine grey hair that hangs over a thin shallow face.

'At last I look upon your wretched face and see the haggard body of an old bag lady and I feel no pity, for you deserved your sad empty life and have no right to claim it back. You betrayed my brother and sent him to hell where he's waiting for you. I feel his pain every second for we were born into the world together and are bound together and even though we are parted, our souls remain as one. You took my beloved twin brother from me and now you'll pay the final price by joining him in the fires of hell.'

'He deserved his fate along with the rest of you. You dare speak of betrayal when your family betrayed me and stole my life and that of another innocent all in the name of greed. Your brother had a murderous heart and redemption isn't his or yours to claim, but I deserve a second chance of happiness and I claim that right in this court.'

The old woman pauses for a few seconds and then looks up at the **Angel of Judgement**, who's been watching and listening as these bitter tortured spirits tear at each other with venomous rage. 'Have I not endured enough in my eighty-five years on earth?' she pleads. 'I've prayed for so long for God to come and take me and give me the peace I've longed for. Will he not now answer my prayers and give me back my name so that I can finally rest in peace?'

'There are no innocents in this court,' the angel replies as he looks down upon the old woman before turning to Charity, saying in a softer more forgiving tone, 'You've the power of the angels within you, Charity, and you've been charged to speak for your client. What do you say in her defence?'

All eyes are upon her as she feels the full weight of this heavy burden. She contemplates everything that's passed in this Court of Past Souls as she slowly takes another long look into the hearts of the old woman and the three past souls once more.

'You're right, there are no innocents in this court, but there's still so much that's been unanswered and my vision of the past has only opened the doorway into the knowledge I need to defend my client and so I ask this court for more time before judgement is passed.'

The still sound of silence dominates the room as the old woman and her accusers along with Charity, Sam and Andy await the **Angel of Judgement**'s decision. Charity watches the old woman's face slowly disintegrate as the last drop of hope ebbs away, while her accusers stand under the shadow of the angel's magnificent wings, smiling that smug grin of satisfaction, convinced that her fate will be as theirs. If only they could feel compassion and forgiveness, she thinks to herself, then all of them would be set free, but still, after all these years of wandering in the darkness of the spirit world, they've learnt nothing. To forgive rather than accuse is the purest sign of

19

enlightenment. Through the Court of Past Souls, they've been given the opportunity by God's mighty messenger to go through the doorway of enlightenment and finally reach the gateway to the afterlife.

The silence is finally broken as the room is filled with the voice of God's mighty angel:

'Your words are spoken wisely, Charity, and time will be offered to you to go through the doorway of the past and seek out the knowledge that'll bring the guilty to justice and set the innocent free. At the beginning of this court you were given a date: **21st June 1940**. I now give you another: **15th August 1945**. Each date will open and close the gateway to the past, which will enable you to return to this court and speak the final words necessary to defend your client. You'll return to this court on **15th August** – three weeks from now when Final Judgement will be passed.'

On those fatal words he spreads his magnificent blood-red wings high into the air, then draws down encircling them around the three past souls as he scoops them up and they disappear into nothingness, leaving behind the old woman, whose dead body is back in the refrigeration unit awaiting her final fate on **15th August**.

Andy nervously opens the refrigeration door to check that the old woman's body is still there. Sam and Charity stand beside him as he pulls back the white sheet to see her motionless corpse lying there. Sam makes sure she's well back this time for she has no intention of being grabbed a second time; the vision of trying to release herself from the clutches of the last body Charity and she visited in a morgue is still vivid in her memory. As the three of them stare intensely at her body, they feel strangely calm and unafraid, for what they see is a very frail old lady, whose face shows the pitiful signs of a woman who died as she lived: lonely and sad.

'Looking at her now,' says Sam, 'you'd never believe she was capable of the terrible things those nasty spirits accused her of, betrayal, deceit, lies, lust and stealing. I mean, she looks so frail and withered that you can't imagine her being young and as wicked as they claim. I don't believe them; they were really unpleasant and I reckon they're the wicked ones and she's had her life destroyed by them. What do think, Charity? What did you see when you put your hand through that horrible spirit's body? It makes me shudder all over just thinking about it. I'm glad you're the inceptor and not me because there's no way you'd catch me putting my hand through any spirits.'

Andy pulls the white sheet over her head and puts her corpse back into the refrigeration unit as the three of them return to his office where Sam makes some tea and coffee.

'You've not said much or answered my question, old girl, what's going on in that head of yours?' Sam asks, slightly puzzled, as she passes out the biscuits. The three of them sit silently drinking and munching in the stillness of the morgue. Finally the silence is broken as Andy asks:

'Does that mean the angel and so-called past souls will be back again on **15th August** (sniff, sniff), because I don't think her body will still be here (sniff, sniff)? I mean, basically she's a Jane Doe, which means the hospital will discharge the body within the next seven days (sniff, sniff) and she'll get a pauper's funeral by the Co-op, who'll claim the money back from the State (sniff, sniff). So how will you defend her if her body isn't here (sniff, sniff)?'

Sam and Andy glance at each other, perplexed at her silence.

'Hello, anyone in there,' Sam enquires as she taps Charity's forehead.

'Sorry, old girl, my thoughts were cocooned in another world, but I'm back now. Don't worry, Andy, angels and spirits aren't governed by mortal time or places. They'll find the old woman and us wherever we are. My concern is the **15th** is but a whisper of time away and the journey I've to make into the past to unlock the truth is an epic one. In my vision we have to go back sixty-five years to the dark days of World War II and cross the Atlantic to another country, Canada to discover what evil deeds were perpetrated by the tortured spirits held in the Court of Past Souls and what sins, if any, were committed by the old woman.'

'What did you see in your vision that connects the old woman with Canada and the War?' Sam asks now completely enthralled.

'The vision was broken like a jigsaw puzzle with many of the pieces missing so it won't be easy to unravel the mystery behind the old woman's past, and there's, I fear, a terrible dark secret that our accusing past souls don't want uncovered. But there's other secrets as well, which great and powerful men in dark suits collaborated together on; my gift tells me these were performed in the name of war and carried out in great danger. They saved the British nation in its battle against Hitler, but like all dark secrets, there are two sides and they could easily have destroyed it. This great secret lasted throughout the war years and beyond. It involved the collaboration of another great nation, Canada, where deep underground another world existed, unknown, except for a chosen few. Somewhere within these intertwined underworlds other dark deeds were done, which involved our old woman and her accusers. To uncover their hidden secrets I'll need to travel back to the dark days of war and across the Atlantic and the only clues are two dates: **21st June 1940** and **15th August 1945**.'

'Wow, no wonder you were silent for so long; that's some jigsaw puzzle to piece together,' says Sam, fiddling with her dressing-gown and still feeling uncomfortable even though the only other people in the room, apart from Andy and Charity, are corpses, none of whom are interested in her fashion sense.

'Where do you begin, Miss Holmes (sniff, sniff)? It seems an almost impossible task (sniff, sniff) and surely God (sniff, sniff), who sees all and knows everything, must know their secrets (sniff, sniff); so why doesn't he just punish the guilty and set the innocent free?' asks Andy, who's seen the wonders of the spirit world through Charity, but still can't comprehend its cruel and sometimes evil battle for redemption and truth, where the spirits tear at each other in their fight for power in this infinite and sometimes abominable world.

'The spirit world's no different from the mortal world, Andy,' Charity replies. 'Sometimes to achieve your desires in the mortal world you'll journey along a difficult path, which will test not only your physical and mental abilities, but also your inner soul. It's your soul that God looks into and which, depending upon the choices you've made and the deeds you've perpetrated, will be either your punishment or redemption when entering the world of spirits. Sometimes you'll make choices that'll go against your inner soul, which will be the catalyst to your undoing in your mortal life. Where evil is not always committed in the name of personal desires, but out of necessity. When it's your turn to pass through the gateway into the spirit world, God looks into your soul and sees all of your secrets, and judgement is passed, but he's the One True Being and has compassion. So although he can give absolution, sometimes the souls before him must earn it and be truly repentant for their sins. Not all souls are able to do this yet they're not evil, just lost and need guidance to show them the right path to enable them to enter the afterlife. The Court of Past Souls is their chance to right their wrongs, but only if their true souls are intrinsically good, which God already knows. He will afford all souls, even the dark ones, one last chance to right their wrongs. I've been chosen as the Inceptor, who'll intercept between the old woman and her accusers, who've yet to earn absolution and be truly repentant. They had an opportunity in the court today to show their true souls, but still they cling onto the past and are unable to let go, so I've been chosen to bring the past into the present and lay it before them. They must look into the abyss of their past lives and open up their true selves and repent for their past deeds, which will afford them passage into the afterlife. Or if they deny their guilt, they will remain in the Middle Life as tortured spirits or, depending on how dark their true souls really are, be sent into the eternal flames of the Dark Life. What they won't be able to do is hide the truth as God is all-seeing, so there you have it, Andy, it is indeed a quest of epic proportions, but one that I must accept otherwise these four souls will not be afforded their last chance at redemption.'

Both Andy and Sam glance at each other apprehensively, for listening to Charity has brought their own inner souls into question. What necessitates a dark soul and what judgement will be made of the paths they've chosen during their mortal lives?

'It makes you afraid to look into yourself for fear of what you might see, yet if you don't, you'll never really know if you've chosen the right path.' Sam comments, suddenly aware that perhaps vanity and selfishness are qualities she's not thought too deeply about before.

'Yes, Miss Holmes (sniff, sniff), who's really bad and who's innocent (sniff, sniff). Surely it's not that simple (sniff, sniff)?' Andy laments, suddenly aware of his own mortality and inner soul.

Charity grins widely, showing her slightly imperfect white teeth that light up her pale Irish complexion and sparkling blue eyes as she throws back her head, tossing her blonde hair over her shoulders. She sees the fear on her two friends' faces as they suddenly picture their future in the spirit world, which somehow doesn't look that rosy now.

'Don't worry,' she replies, laughing infectiously, 'the Court of Past Souls only stands for those souls who've crossed over into the wrong paths during their mortal lives, which doesn't apply to you two.'

They both breathe a sigh of relief at Charity's gentle reassurance that their place in the afterlife is 'booked in' so to speak.

'Where do you begin your journey into the past, Miss Holmes (sniff, sniff)? And will you have enough time (sniff, sniff)?'

Charity pauses for a few moments as her mind ponders on the daunting challenge that's been bestowed upon her before answering: 'At the beginning of course?'

'But where's that?' Sam asks.

'At the birth,' replies Charity, enjoying winding the two of them up with her cryptic replies.

'What birth?' retorts Sam, slightly agitated at Charity's one syllable answers.

'The birth of the old woman, whose path crossed over into that of the three past souls where war and the hand of fate crossed their paths with the powerful men in dark suits, whose "secret" corrupted their souls and changed their destiny for ever.'

'But surely their destiny was already written?' interrupts Sam, remembering how Charity's destiny as an inceptor was already foretold together with the RING's and

Andy's when they battled the Dark One at the Final Reckoning.

'You're right, Sam, but destiny can be altered through free will, which God gave to everyone and allows us to make our own choices. Sometimes the dark side of human nature is so powerful that it awakens the beast within us, which is only separated by the thin line of our own conscience. This can so easily be corrupted if fate and opportunity cross our paths, blinding our judgement and altering our destiny forever. My vision showed that fate and opportunity crossed the paths of these four souls, simultaneously awakening their own inner beasts, where darkness and evil triumphed.'

They all sit silently for a moment remembering how easy it is for evil to manifest itself should the good stand by and do nothing, while the bad sow their seed of destruction.

'Andy, my good friend, it's time for me to begin my quest, so I must bid you farewell and thanks for everything,' says Charity softly.

'That's it, Miss Holmes (sniff, sniff)? You don't need me for anything else (sniff, sniff)?'

'Your destiny was fulfilled the moment you took this job and our paths crossed again, but now it's my turn to fulfil my destiny, so stop worrying, my dear friend, and continue your work in peace.'

Andy sighs with relief at surviving his encounter with the spirit world as he waves goodbye to Charity and Sam. Secretly he's sad to see them go as no one has ever treated him with such kindness and respect. They make their way back down the dark corridor and into the lift. As Sam tries desperately not to look at her reflection in the mirror for fear of her inner soul being tainted and Charity fumbles in her bag for her mobile to contact Monty, darkness suddenly descends upon them and the lift screeches to a halt. They both stand motionless with their eyes darting everywhere, unable to see in the pitch-black, claustrophobic, and now eerily silent lift.

Charity fumbles around in her bag to find her keys where there's a tiny torch attached to the key-ring. She flashes it around the lift looking for the emergency button. Finally she locates it.

'Hello, anybody there, we're trapped in the lift? Can you hear us? I repeat, we're trapped in the lift and need help.'

'Why isn't anybody answering?' cries Sam, who by now is beginning to panic. If there's one thing Sam is sure of it's to always expect the unexpected when you're around Charity. For demons and spirits have walked the earth since before man, and their power is all consuming and relentless. There's nowhere to hide when they seek you out and unless you have exceptional powers like Charity, no protection. Since the Final Reckoning where Charity and the RING defeated the Devil, his children (the Dark Trio) and his evil demons and spirits, his quest for revenge is merciless and unremitting with only one outcome: the destruction of his mortal enemy Charity and the ultimate prize: his rebirth into the mortal world. Charity and the RING destroyed his 'children' so the war continues, where everyday she and her 'family' (the RING) battle against the evil demons and spirits of the Dark Life to protect the mortal world from eternal darkness.

'What are we going to do? I've a bad feeling that something terrible is about to happen.'

'We do nothing, for there's nowhere to run to.' Charity tries to remain calm for Sam's sake although deep in the pit of her stomach she feels the same fear.

'Well that's a great comfort, do nothing! I feel absolutely fine now that I know we're trapped in this horrific nightmare and there's no way out. I'll just stand here in my dressing-gown waiting for...'

'Quiet, Sam, I feel a presence.'

Suddenly as the two of them cling onto each other, the lift begins to move not downwards or upwards, but from within. The walls start bulging outwards towards them forming shape-shifting ghostly apparitions like black treacle with no faces that cry and moan as they move closer and closer to Charity and Sam, attaching themselves to their bodies.

'Oh my God, they're all over me, burning into my skin.' screams Sam as the demon spirits liquefy themselves into her skin, slowly covering her entire body in their black shape-shifting treacle, devouring her until eventually she'll be no more.

'Help me, Charity, help me.'

'Close your eyes, Sam, and hold your breath. I know you are there, Lucifer. Show yourself or are you so afraid to face me on your own that you need to send these pitiful creatures in your stead.'

She continues trying to bait her enemy to come forth in the hope that he'll release the demon shape-shifting entities, giving her the opportunity to think of another way out. Suddenly just before their entire bodies are devoured they feel the black treacle slipping from them and slowly returning into the walls as the lift takes on another presence. This time the lift begins to shake uncontrollably as the floor beneath opens up into an endless black hole. They cling onto the walls, standing on their toes with barely any room for movement.

'Well that's done a lot of good,' bleats Sam as she desperately tries to maintain the inner steel she so admires in Charity.

'There's no satisfying you at times, old girl,' retorts Charity as her brain goes into overdrive trying to think of a way out.

Suddenly the fires of hell erupt from beneath the black

hole, almost touching their terrified faces, as the Prince of Darkness rises from his kingdom. They watch as he slowly emerges from beneath what seems an endless pit of fire and darkness that engulfs the lift completely, taking them into another dimension: his world. Flapping his huge bat wings behind him, the Horned Goat of Mendes, half man, half beast, pierces them with his dark satanic eyes as he floats in mid air with his goat's head and inverted horns, black hairy human body, hoofed legs and tail.

'You try to trick me, Charity!' The demonic hollow words echo around them. 'I know your thoughts and can destroy you at any time, but it pleases me to see you and your pathetic family squirm! Your souls are mine for the taking, for no power in this world is greater than mine. Come with me now, Charity, and feel the pleasures and power of the Dark Life.'

'You think I don't know you, Lucifer,' she retaliates, bravely. Sam clings onto her so tightly that she can feel the blood flow stop in her arm. 'I knew you'd come, for vanity was always one of your greatest weaknesses and the sin that finally expelled you into the hell you now pathetically call your kingdom.'

'Brave but foolish words, for no inceptor is powerful enough to defeat me. I can destroy you and your sad little friend with just a thought.'

The flames of hell erupt like a volcano, almost engulfing Charity and Sam within them. But Charity holds firm, for she has the infallible power of thought; she can penetrate the minds of demons and spirits to see their visions and use her thoughts to defeat or destroy them. The mighty Archangel Focus bestowed this gift upon her after the Final Reckoning.

'If that were so, I'd be yours long ago, but the truth is purity of thought can't be destroyed by you or your demons as your servants must come willingly otherwise they're neither spirits of heaven or hell, but lost souls of the Middle Life. What good is a kingdom without the servants to rule over and do your bidding?'

'Why should I care whether your soul is mine or lost in the Middle Life? Your destruction will be enough.'

Charity smiles, for she knows that unless her soul is completely his she'll always pose a threat even as a lost soul in the Middle Life. Standing erect, she faces her enemy head on as Sam cowers beneath him with her eyes closed awaiting her fate. As their eyes meet their minds penetrate each other speaking without words, battling for supremacy. Their thoughts whisper in the air, while all around them the fires of hell continue to erupt and they float in the endless pit of evil.

'Come to me, Charity, join me in my kingdom. You know you can't resist for your destiny is the Dark Life. Don't fight me, Charity, hear my voice and feel my power. Embrace the world of darkness. Come, Charity, join me, join me.'

The words float inside her mind, tormenting her with their relentless whispering, over and over again willing her to join him as she fights to keep control of her thoughts. Little by little she takes command, spitting back his words through her infallible power of thought.

'Darkness isn't my kingdom, nor are you my Lord. There is only One True Being and you're not he. Be gone, thou evil spirit, for your thoughts are not mine.'

She repeats her final words over and over again, banishing him from her mind until he no longer holds her in the power of his thoughts.

'You will come to me Charity. It's your destiny.'

The words ricochet through the lift as he looses his power over her and returns into the flaming fires of the Dark Life until all that's left is an empty lift carrying two slightly dishevelled, but triumphant females.

The lift door opens and light returns as they make

their way along the corridor, finally collapsing on Sam's lumpy, but very welcome bed.

'And where have you been, Mrs Francis, for yah shouldn't be walking around having just had your operation this morning,' says the stern ward sister, a tall plain looking woman with a thin pale face and badly dyed black hair. She takes her temperature and checks her chart before stomping off after telling her she's free to go home the next morning.

'Well I won't be sorry to see the back of this place, and next time I need to come into hospital, don't visit me, OK!' bleats Sam as she repairs her image, having forgotten all about her inner soul.

'Don't worry, I won't, one corpse and one demonic devil is enough for any thoughtful friend to deal with in a day's visit.' It's 6 p.m. and the dinner trolley comes round. 'I'll just go and get a bite to eat while you tuck into your plate of delicious plastic food.' Charity leaves Sam prodding away at her dinner with her fork as she makes her way down to the first floor (by the steps, bypassing the lift) to the cafeteria. She orders sandwiches and tea, and phones Monty on her mobile.

'Hi, honey, just phoning to let you know Sam's OK and will be discharged tomorrow morning.'

On the other end Monty picks up the extension in the library at their London house where he's catching up on some reading after an eventful day interrogating 'industrial spies' at Special Operations secret headquarters, where he works for the British government.

'That's great news, Spud, so when do you think you'll be home?'

'In a couple of hours. Tell Aunt Lizzy not to bother with dinner as I've just had a sandwich.

'Hmm, she won't like that, you know how she fusses over you.'

'I know but I'm not that hungry.'

Immediately Monty senses something's up as he sits upright in his leather chair by the fire discarding his book.

'What's happened, Spud? I can hear it in your voice and feel it in your heartbeat.'

'Are you sure you haven't got any psychic powers that you're not telling me about. You seem to be able to read my mind more and more lately,' jokes Charity.

'Over a decade of living with you and fighting demons and spirits, something's bound to rub off eventually, besides I always know when you've been "called upon" – your voice changes and your soul touches mine; it's kismet; we feel as one.'

Charity smiles to herself as she listens to his deep gentle voice enveloping her in his protective love, which no matter how many times she hears it always catches her breath and steals her heart. She whispers into the phone. 'I've been charged with a quest to save the soul of an old woman, but there isn't much time, my love.'

She can hear him laughing away at the other end as he replies. 'Well, no surprises there. Every tortured spirit that seeks your help is always somehow pressed for time; it seems the spirit world isn't that much different from the mortal one.' He jokes, but inside he's worried for he knows Charity's not telling him everything and he feels her fear just as acutely as he feels her love.

'We are a wit tonight,' she laughs. 'I'll see you soon, honey, and I love you.'

She makes her way back to Sam and says goodnight before driving off into the mist of the night, contemplating in the silence of her car the epic journey that lies ahead.

4

Secrets of the Dead

As Charity places her car keys in the silver tray on the table in the entrance hall, she breathes a sigh of relief. She looks around her capacious Victorian home, with its several floors, including a basement flat (where her niece Robyn lives), and the beautiful antique furniture and ornaments that she and Monty have collected during their travels over the years, and she thinks to herself what a privileged life she now lives and how far removed it is from the poor Irish immigrant East End background she was born into. The old woman crosses her mind as she ponders on the hard life she must have had living rough on the streets, and yet somewhere deep in the past Charity's gift of 'Clear Seeing' tells her that she once lived in a house just like hers.

'Come on now, my darling, what are you doing standing in the hallway? Get yourself in here with your family and I'll make yah some warm soup and a nice strong cup of tea,' roars Aunt Lizzy from the kitchen where Monty, Jack and Robyn are sitting drinking tea.

'You look tired, Spud,' Monty says lovingly as he gently kisses her on the lips. Aunt Lizzy dishes up a bowl of her thick vegetable soup with a couple of slices of buttered toast and a large mug of tea.

'Get stuck into that, my girl, and you'll be just fine.'

'Thanks, Lizzy, you're a gem,' Charity says as she tucks into the soup. She relays her day to the others who listen intently as Aunt Lizzy fusses around as usual.

'Do you think we'll ever be free of Lucifer or is our life going to be one long endless battle with the Lord of Darkness and his evil demons?' sighs Robyn as Charity brings them up to speed with her latest encounter.

'Well he's been around at lot longer than us I'm afraid and he's a bit of a sore loser,' quips Jack in that rugged ex-SAS army manner of his (though underneath he's a marshmallow to his 'adopted' family). He brushes back his thick mop of brown hair, while smiling that cheeky manly grin of his.

'I'm afraid it's my destiny though sometimes it feels more like a curse, which unfortunately you've all inherited by association and for which I'll always feel culpable,' replies Charity, who carries a great burden of guilt in her heart at putting her beloved family and friends (the RING) in such interminable and constant danger through her vocation as the Inceptor.

'Whatever destiny has in store for us I know one thing for sure, it would be an empty existence without you by my side and certainly a lot duller, and if fighting Lucifer and his demons is part of the package then so be it,' says Monty as he puts his arms around Charity and squeezes her tight towards him. Inside he's fearful for her and worries constantly that one day Lucifer will win and claim his beautiful and brave wife's soul and she'll be lost to him for ever.

'Enough talk of demons and devils now, for I'll not have them spoiling our evening,' growls Aunt Lizzy protectively as she sees Charity looking tired and vulnerable.

'You're right, Lizzy,' replies Monty, leading the way into the lounge where they all settle down for the evening as Jack performs his favourite job of the day, serving up the drinks. While they all wallow in the warmth and safety of their little piece of heaven it's not long before the conversation gets round to their new quest: the old woman.

'It's a tall order tracing the old woman, for anybody that's lived on the streets as long as she has really does become invisible.'

'Well, that's positive thinking, Jack, I feel so much better now,' joke's Charity as she snuggles up on the couch with Monty.

'I don't mean to sound negative, but people who live on the streets don't want to be found and become nameless and faceless and after a while invisible. It could take months or even years to find out anything, and according to you we've only got until fifteenth August – literally three weeks,' grumbles Jack as he helps himself to another malt whisky.

'I'm afraid I tend to agree with Jack. After all we haven't much to go on; in fact we know nothing at all about her,' says Monty ruefully.

'But we do know something,' snaps Charity rather defensively.

'Like what?' asks Robyn.

'Her home, the very streets she hid in and the people she lived amongst; they're like a brotherhood that's separate from the rest of us, protecting and looking after each other. Somewhere out there in those dark streets someone knew about her and that's where we'll begin.'

'Surely to God you're not going to mix with the down and outs living in those filthy hovels full of rats and diseases. I'll not have yah bringing any germs and the likes back here,' shrieks Aunt Lizzy.

'Shame on you, Lizzy, they're just people like us only not as fortunate and there but for the grace of God et cetera, et cetera,' retorts Charity, feeling a little disappointed in her lack of compassion.

'I didn't mean it like that, my darling, of course I feel sorry for those poor souls, but it doesn't mean I'd want to serve them dinner,' she replies, feeling somewhat shameful at her harsh words, while everyone else has a little giggle at the thought of her serving dinner to a smelly tramp.

'Joking apart, we can begin the TIE by tracing her last movements when she was admitted to hospital. Someone there must know something of her habits as she was a regular patient over the years and she must've had some belongings on her, which may give us a clue to her past. When I go back to pick Sam up in the morning I'll do a bit of detective work.' The TIE is Charity's *modus operandi*: trace, investigate and eliminate.

'Where's Leo, isn't he picking her up?' Robyn asks.

'He's in court first thing so I've volunteered to drive Sam home, which will fit in nicely with doing a bit of sleuthing.'

'What about the rest of us, Spud? What's ticking away in that little psychic brain of yours?' Monty quips knowing full well that Charity's already thought things through and has come up with a strategy to uncover the mystery of the old woman.

'Well we know that whatever happened to change the destiny of the old woman it began on **21st June 1940** and ended on **15th August 1945**, which the Angel of Judgement said opened and closed the gateway to the past. Something catastrophic happened in war time that somehow crossed over into the paths of the old woman and the three past souls, which resulted in her becoming "invisible" and hiding something that they wanted. Also in the court the daughter mentioned her twin brother, whose soul is in hell, but who the old woman said had a murderous heart. She also said that there was another "innocent" involved. So we have two more past souls who've also crossed the path of the old woman. Then there are the powerful men in dark suits collaborating behind closed doors who have a dark secret to do with the war. These men are in collusion with other men in pinstriped suits in the City, who in turn somehow end up across the waters in Canada, where deep underground they're guarding something very secretive, which the powerful men in dark suits instigated. Somehow all these elements are connected, some by cunning and manipulative planning and others by fate or chance, which ultimately led to the downfall of the old woman and all the other past souls.'

'That's some enigma to unravel.'

'I know honey, it's some puzzle, isn't it? And one that when we fit all the pieces together will tell an amazing story.'

'Wow, I can't wait to get started. What do you want me to do?' shrieks Robyn who suddenly feels a tremendous rush of adrenaline running through her as her imagination goes into overdrive.

'Start by checking all the hostels and shelters within say a ten mile radius of the hospital plus all the charities that provide food, clothing and support to the homeless. She must've stayed or eaten at some of these places during her years on the streets and hopefully someone will know something about her or at least provide us with a clue so we can trace her origins. That should keep you busy for a while.'

'You're not kidding! Did I say I couldn't wait to get started?' Robyn groans, suddenly realising the avalanche of phone calls and paperwork ahead of her.

'I'm intrigued by your vision of these powerful men having clandestine meetings in covert places and then colluding with others to form what I suspect is an illegal or unofficial alliance with other powerful forces in Canada in the name of war,' Monty says, looking very perplexed as Jack chips in:

'Yeah and didn't you mention that you saw something else in the water, Miss Charity?'

'British battleships, which my gift of sight tells me were being used not only to go into battle, but also to carry something top secret, which had nothing to do with weapons. I also felt that only a chosen few on the ships actually knew what they were carrying and would go so far as to say that this was a mission involving subterfuge and skulduggery, but at the same time was instrumental in enabling the British, in collaboration with the Canadians, to win the war against Hitler.'

Everyone is silent as they slowly begin to realise they're about to embark on a journey of discovery that will open up a Pandora's box of dark deeds and secrets, which will bring forth the evil that men do in the name of war.

'This is a job for Jack and me,' Monty says as his whole body becomes alive with the thought of uncovering some dark government secret involving high-ranking civil servants or, as his gut instincts are telling him, which could possibly go all the way up to the prime minister, Churchill himself.

Charity can feel his body quivering with excitement as Jack leaps of his chair, pacing the room, his deep-set blue-green eyes alight with passion as he brushes back his thick mop of brown hair revealing the scar over his left eyebrow.

'This could be big, Monty, I've a feeling about it; a covert operation involving the British government, the Navy, powerful businessmen and the Canadian government all working together in the name of war.'

'But where does the old woman come into it?' butts in Robyn, tossing back her long, silky, black hair as she continues. 'I hate to spoil the moment, but it does sound a bit far fetched, I mean she was just an old bag lady living rough on the streets and now all of a sudden we're into covert operations involving the government.'

'Ah, but was she?' says Aunt Lizzy, suddenly, in her no nonsense Irish brogue.

'What do you mean, Lizzy?'

'I mean we don't know anything about her, Robyn, my darling, which means she could have been a spy or government agent who had to go into hiding for all number of reasons. She chose to disappear so was either running from something or hiding something. Either way she wasn't just a nobody.'

All eyes turn to Aunt Lizzy, stunned by her cool yet apt clarification of the situation.

'Well put Lizzy,' says Charity. 'I keep remembering her words at the hospital. "They want what I know but I was too clever for them and made myself invisible and they'll never find it now. I win, I win, they lose, they lose." We need to find out what it was "they" wanted and if "they" were her accusers, the past souls, or others? Either way, you're right, Lizzy, she wasn't just a bag lady, but somebody who, as she admitted in court, "did wrong but learnt from the experts". Who were the experts and what did she mean by "did wrong"?'

'That's settled then, Spud,' says Monty firmly. 'Jack and I will use our connections in the government and Secret Service, where deep in the archives there must be a record of what happened on those two dates.'

'But if it was all covert and illicit then it won't be recorded anywhere will it?' Robyn asks, slightly confused.

'Trust me, Robyn, no matter how secret or clandestine an operation, someone somewhere always writes it down especially if it's to do with the government. Red tape will always catch them out in the end and Jack and I are dab hands at digging up other people's dirt,' Monty replies, while Jack grins and nods his head in agreement.

'Well that just leaves me, what's my job, Charity, my darling?' asks Aunt Lizzy, who by now has changed her opinion of the old woman and feels that she's got quite a history behind her.

'When I arrived home tonight there was a moment when I was standing in the hallway and I felt her entity within me, where I felt that she once lived in a house like this, but wasn't the mistress. In the court the wife said they took her in and gave her shelter so she probably worked for them in return for room and board.'

'Leave it to me, Charity, my darling,' interrupts Aunt Lizzy, all excited now that she's got a project to get her teeth into. 'I'll do a bit of sleuthing myself and see what I can find out from my friends and contacts in the service industry. When you've been a housekeeper for as long as I have, my darling, you get to know everybody's business, for gossip is the food of life to those who work for the rich and powerful.'

A wonderful sense of tranquility comes over everyone as they settle back for the evening contemplating their separate tasks in the first stages of the TIE, yet each is simmering with excitement as their brains tick away trying to piece together the various scenarios of the old woman's life. Did she work for her accusers and if so what job did she do? What did she discover or find that they wanted so desperately that she had to go into hiding? What dark deed did they commit that ultimately denied their souls entry into the afterlife? Was she a spy or secret agent or were they? What connection did they or she have with these powerful men in the government and how did the British battleships and a secret underground building across the Atlantic in Canada connect with her and her accusers?

5

The Power of Thor

It's just past midnight as they all make their way to bed:
Robyn to her flat in the basement and Jack and Aunt
Lizzy to their rooms in the large Victorian house that
was once full of servants, whom Charity sometimes sees
during the long nights when she walks the hallways unable
to sleep before settling down in her 'quiet room'. Souls
from the spirit world who come to her through the
'Doorway of Psychic Dreams' as they float past her in
the darkness of night; some are happy others sad as they
whisper their secrets about the previous masters of 29
Chalfont Square. She's not afraid of her 'hallway spirits'
as they mean her no harm, but just want to tell her of
bygone days when grand and sumptuous parties were
held and where those upstairs were waited on by those
downstairs, who watched in awe and envy at the glittering
world of the rich and powerful. The moment Charity
entered 29 Chalfont Square she felt its soul calling to
her as her hallway spirits whispered their approval of the
new mistress of the house.

'Do you think you'll be able to sleep, Spud, or will the
spirits be calling to you through the doorway again tonight?'
Monty asks, as they get ready for bed. He's noticed she's
been more restless than usual and more often than not he
wakes to find an empty space beside him.

'Lately the hallway spirits have been more active and I haven't been able to discover why, but ever since the old woman called to me I've realised they've been trying to help me. She's entered their world now and is calling to them for help and I feel them all around me trying to pass on her messages.'

Monty looks puzzled. 'I don't understand, Spud, why send a message to you through the spirits of our house? Why couldn't she tell you direct either in the hospital ward or through the Court of Past Souls? Why go through them?'

Charity smiles that quiet knowing smile of hers as she replies, 'Spirits are the same as mortals; they seek out those who are similar to themselves where they feel safe and secure, which is what the old woman's done. She's sought out the lost souls who were once servants in the mortal world and found those who once worked in this house, who in turn have been waiting for her, which is why they've been restless lately. They've been waiting for her to contact them so they can help me to help her and in doing so will seek redemption and peace for themselves. In the spirit world there's a never ending wheel that's constantly turning. The lost souls try to leap off this wheel of eternal emptiness into the peace and tranquility of the afterlife.'

Now it's Monty's turn to smile as he says, 'No different from the constant wheel of life here on earth then.'

'Got it in one, honey, sometimes the thin line that separates us mortals from those in spirit is so fine that it's almost tangible, which is why these unhappy souls often walk this thin line between our two worlds treading the wheel of eternity, never knowing how or when to stop so they can move on to their rightful place in the afterlife.'

'Well I'm switching off my earthly wheel right now for

these old bones are too weary to keep turning,' jokes Monty as he kisses Charity goodnight before the two of them turn out the lights and close the door on another eventful day in the lives of the Holmes.

It's 4 a.m. and Charity's restless and unable to sleep as she tosses and turns, her mind alive with the whispering sounds of the lost souls calling to her through the doorway of her dreams, begging her to help them. The whispers get louder and louder until she can stand it no longer and once again rises to walk amongst the spirits of the night who bring her messages from the other side.

While she makes her way along the long hallway to the 'quiet room' a chilling coldness fills the air. The blackness of the night becomes a translucent mist that moves like a twisting serpent, winding its way through the darkness from within the hollowness of the walls until finally she sees in the distance the 'Black Door of Death'.

The black and white stone floor beneath her begins to move as she looks down to see it transforming into a pool of blood that separates, forming a pathway with borders of black carnations on either side leading to the Doorway of Death. Her heart stops as the door begins to open for this is a dark place and one that shouldn't be entered for once the door closes behind you there's no escape.

Charity's never seen this vision before, but her fear is real for legend has it that should you see the 'Black Door of Death' and it opens before you then the eternal darkness of death is your fate. Although she's not moving, the door appears to be getting closer and closer as the blood red pathway beneath her moves, slowly towards it, while the heavy black door opens wider and wider, drawing her into the endless blackness that lies beyond. No matter how hard she tries to escape, the pathway won't allow her to leave and keeps moving forward, while she struggles to avoid her fate.

'What is it that you want from me?' she yells as the Doorway of Death is almost upon her. 'This isn't my destiny for my soul's not dark and I refuse to enter. This vision isn't real and I challenge the entity that's created it to come forth and reveal who it is now. I call upon the Angels of the Light to protect me.'

She repeats her words over and over again, waiting for the vision to disappear, while fearful of the entity that's created it and praying for her protectors to come and save her. Suddenly the door opens wide but instead of drawing her into the void she sees a figure walking towards her from out of the darkness of eternal death. Her body is being pulled backwards by an unseen force. As the figure draws closer she sees it's a man aged about 25 years and walks with a pride and arrogance that she's seen before. He has a thin, shallow face with cold, dark eyes and thin, wispy brown hair that's parted in the middle and greased back, giving him an uncompromising appearance. A cold shiver runs down the back of her spine as he draws closer. Suddenly she feels the familiar presence of her protectors behind her. She turns to see Ma and Pa moving towards her until finally they're standing by her side. It was them she felt pulling her backwards, forcing the evil spirit behind the door to come forth and reveal itself.

To her right stands her father, now a mighty guardian angel with his magnificent pale-blue wings that are folded behind him trailing onto the floor. She looks into his handsome face and feels the power of his protection. To her left stands her mother, a beautiful Angel of Divine Intervention with her magnificent white wings, long flowing hair and pure white translucent body floating beside her as she gently holds her hand and whispers, 'Don't be afraid, my darling, you've called upon our Lord for his protection and he hears you. Feel the light of his love and our strength and know that no evil can survive the purity of heaven's light.'

As her mother's voice drifts into the air she hears the strong protective words of her father. 'The malevolent spirit that tried to draw you into the eternal darkness fears your gift and has risen from the Dark Life to stop you discovering the truth, for his soul is evil and seeks revenge upon your charge, the old woman, who condemned him to his fate. There's no redemption, for his crime is of the most heinous kind and he feels no remorse, only hate. Should you succeed in your quest, my beloved daughter, then he'll never taste the sweetness of revenge, which is all that his dark soul yearns for. Fight him, my darling, and let love and truth be your armour against this demoniacal being.'

Just as her father's words trickle from his lips the spirit is upon them.

'Your pathetic little hallway spirits who hang around their past lives trying to capture lost dreams fought a fruitless battle to keep me out, for their powers are useless against that of the Dark One, whose reach is endless.'

His voice is sharp and heartless and instantly Charity knows he's the twin brother who was betrayed by the old woman. His body is not ravaged with the pain of old age like his sister, the old woman's accuser in the Court of Past Souls, but young and in its prime. Charity, with her gift of 'Clear Seeing', can see deep into his tortured soul: he's constantly at the mercy of his demonic master the Prince of Darkness, Lucifer, who calls upon him to do his bidding; his lugubrious life as his eternal servant is his punishment. Although he mocks her hallway spirits she sees his real torment and knows that he'd trade places with them instantly to escape the

45

nefarious and vile existence his condemned soul now has to endure.

'You may ridicule the spirits who walk in the shadows and hallways of this house, but I see your true soul and it's envious of their snatched moments of past happiness, which you'll never experience for your fate is an eternity of darkness and servitude to the cruellest of masters, who'll never show you pity or give you release from your eternal prison.' Charity retaliates, as her guardians stand beside her and her hallway spirits appear from within the shadows all around them. Grey wispy figures that fly like missiles in the air as they dart in and out, whispering:

'Leave our house now for you're not welcome; go back through the Doorway of Death from whence you came. We are the spirits of the night who walk the halls and protect our mistress; leave now, dark spirit, or feel our wrath.'

Hundreds of spirits fly through the air, whispering and chanting at their unwelcome visitor as he glares at Charity and her guardians. They remain still, confident in their own powers, while he tries to mask his own fear, for he knows that all their powers combined far outreach his.

Time seems to be motionless as Charity mesmerises him with her eyes, penetrating his mind, trying to read his thoughts by using her powers of infallible thought.

'You'll not read my mind,' he shouts, holding his head between his hands as her powers penetrate his thoughts. 'Protect me, master,' he shouts.

Just when she's about to open the doorway into the dark shadows of his mind she feels an invisible force lifting her in the air, throwing her backwards over the banisters as her body somersaults towards the floor. Suddenly, just before she crashes to the ground, she feels a hand gently grabbing her from behind, carrying her upwards until she's flying high above in the air. Enveloped around her are the magnificent pale-blue wings of her father as he holds her tightly in his arms. Her mother spreads her white wings and flies towards them. They both float bedide her, while the spirits of the house quickly fly around them, forming an impenetrable ring as they hiss and whisper at the evil spirit below.

'Your master has protected you this time,' shouts Charity, 'but he'll not be able to stop me uncovering the truth?'

He looks up at her as she floats in a shield of light, protected by her army of angels and spirits, suddenly realising that this is no weak enemy, but an inceptor of the highest level with the power of the angels behind her. His vision of revenge upon the old woman no longer seems as assured. Charity looks down upon this sad and wretched soul, watching his face crumble before her.

'Why have you come?' she asks, looking deep into his cold eyes to see only darkness and pain staring back at her.

'The old woman's soul belongs to my master and I was sent to bring you that message. She called upon you for help, but retribution will be mine for she betrayed me, stole from me and then condemned my soul for all eternity. I will have my revenge and soon my master will claim what is his, and her final destiny will be fulfilled.'

'You're no innocent, your fate was decided by your own actions and not by another, for your crimes must've been of the most heinous kind for your soul to be condemned to the Dark Life. My charge has been given a second chance and I've been chosen to find the truth. Her life was destroyed and her name taken from her and although this time my powers were weak I will succeed in uncovering the mystery of her past.'

'You dare to judge me when you protect her soul, which was as greedy and envious as mine when we were mortal.

She's no innocent and deserves her fate and I will meet her again on **August 15th**...'

His words disappear into the air as the Black Door of Death opens wide and the evil spirits of the dark fly forth to carry him back into his eternal nightmare. The door and pathway of blood and black carnations are sucked into the walls after him.

'Did you see his face and that terrifying look in his eyes when those evil demon spirits carried him back into his hellish nightmare?' says Charity, with compassion. Even though her gift of sight tells her his soul is dark, her heart can still feel pity for this tortured spirit who'll never know peace. Her guardians spread their wings wide, flapping them up and down as they gently carry her to the ground, while the whispering hallway spirits fly in and round them, laughing and chattering away, happy that their mistress is safe and their 'little piece of heaven' is still intact.

'What's all the noise,' grumbles a dishevelled looking Monty as he enters the hallway in his pyjamas, scratching his unkempt hair. 'Not you lot again, can't a man get any peace in his own house?'

Flying spirits zoom past him, giggling, as he yawns, staring at the two angels floating in the air.

Charity smiles sweetly. 'Sorry, honey, a spot of family business that couldn't wait.'

'I must be the only husband with a houseful of spirits and angels for in-laws who only ever seem to visit in the dead of night.'

Charity and her parents chuckle away as Monty slowly shuffles back to bed, completely unfazed by a house full of ghosts, muttering, 'Hmm, it would be nice if they visited during the day so a man can get some sleep.'

As Monty disappears back to bed, sobriety overtakes the moment as Charity's father turns to her saying softly,

'You must open the portal to the past if you're to beat the clock of time.'

'He's right, my darling,' whispers her mother softly. 'There isn't much time as Lucifer won't wait too long before he strikes again, only next time he won't be so easy to fight off. His hatred of you grows more incessant with each passing moment. Since the battle of the Final Reckoning, your powers have grown and the spirits call upon you more and more for help in protecting them from his evil demons. You've crossed over into his world, and his rage will know no limits, so you must win this battle quickly before he has time to destroy you.'

'The portal to the past – must open the portal,' the spirits whisper as they continue to swoop around in the darkness of the night.

'What's this portal? I've never heard you mention it before?'

'It's a timeless gateway to the past that can only be opened twice every thousand years for eight minutes each time,' her father replies.

'Well that's not much good if time's of the essence,' jokes Charity.

'Ah, but the one thousandth year has come round again,' he says excitedly. 'The portal can be opened when the clock strikes noon on the first day in the eighth month when you can enter the universal gateway to the past. You have twelve hours before you must return at midnight precisely to go back through the Portal to return to your time otherwise you'll be trapped in the past for another thousand years.'

Charity's face lights up as her mind calculates that the first day of the eighth month is one week from now on **Monday 1st August**.

'Where can I find this portal and how do I open it up?' she asks excitedly.

'The power of Thor; you must use your power of "Clear Seeing" through the cards of the mind and soul to show you the way,' her father replies.

'Mind and soul, mind and soul, must use the cards with the power,' the spirits chant as they listen intently, floating in the shadows.

'The ancient cards of the god Thor hold within them the power of infinite sight. They were used by my great grandmother, whose power of "Clear Seeing" was legendary. They were my legacy as the next inceptor in the Merrick family and although I've gazed upon them many times over the years I've never felt worthy enough to follow in her wake and use them in my work. They behold a thousand years of wisdom that only an inceptor with the holy power of the angels within them is powerful and strong enough to use without their magic destroying them.'

'You are that inceptor,' her mother replies as she draws close, wrapping her magnificent white wings around her, cocooning her in a soft, feathered bed of love. 'Look deep within your own soul, my beloved daughter, and you'll see how powerful your gift of sight truly is and that your destiny as her successor can finally be fulfilled.'

'Fulfil your destiny, mistress of the house, behold the cards of infinite sight,' whisper the spirits of the house as their words evaporate into the air while they return to the world of spirits.

'Trust in your powers, beloved daughter, and all will be revealed,' are the final words that flow from her mother's lips as she feels her powerful wings unfold, releasing her from their protective embrace. Her guardians spread their wings and fly up into the heavens, returning to their master, the One True Being.

Charity makes her way to her quiet room to open her sacred tarot chest where she keeps all her treasured cards.

It's a large wooden chest inscribed with ancient carvings depicting God's army of guardian angels who form the 'Circle of Protective Light' around the box. She takes the golden key hidden deep within the pages of the *Sacred Book of Angels* and places it in the lock, turning the key three times anticlockwise while chanting the ancient words of the tarot: '*Taraco Tarusha*' three times. This unlocks the sacred power of the angels who'll protect and guide the Inceptor when they consult the tarot.

While Charity opens her precious chest she carefully searches amongst the many smaller wooden boxes that hold all the different ancient tarot cards wrapped in silk. Also within the chest lie her other precious items: velvet reading cloths and tarot pouches; her crystal ball wrapped in a silk-lined black velvet pouch plus her glass angels, pyramids and crystal stones all wrapped in silk-lined pouches that she's collected in her travels around the world. These are the tools she uses to channel her gift when consulting the ancient tarot.

Finally she comes to the box that holds the cards of the god Thor. A dark, almost black, wooden box, richly carved and inscribed with ancient hieroglyphics that tell the story of their origin, which only an inceptor of the highest order has the knowledge to decipher. Unless the person opening the box can read the ancient inscription aloud without pause or error then entry to the secrets of the cards within is denied. Anyone trying to open the box who doesn't possess the gift of 'sight' will be cursed by Thor, suffer his wrath and be plagued by the three shadows of death: **silence**, the loss of hearing; the **veil**, the loss of sight; and the **withered tongue**, the loss of speech. It's a terrible fate that many who've possessed the box in the past have succumbed to when trying to unlock the power that's held within the cards. Charity carefully lifts the box out of the chest and places it on her desk beside the *Sacred Book of Angels*, which together with the ancient cards of Thor will enable her to open the portal and unlock the mystery of the old woman.

Suddenly a tremendous wave of tiredness comes over her as she feels the heavy burden of failure rush through her body. She contemplates the nightmare of being left behind in another lifetime should anything go wrong when she enters the universal gateway to the past.

'I must be strong and fearless when I evoke the power of Thor.'

She closes the lid, turning the key clockwise three times while chanting the ancient words of the tarot three times before retiring to bed and placing the box and sacred book safely by her bedside. She snuggles up to Monty before falling into a deep and peaceful sleep.

'Good morning, Spud, and I see you've been rummaging again in the night,' he says in his gruff (desperate for a cup of coffee) early morning voice, kissing her on the cheek, while noticing the box and book.

'Morning, honey,' she replies, rubbing her eyes and checking that the book and box are still safe beside her.

'What's the meaning behind these then?' Monty asks, picking up the box.

'Don't touch that,' she yells, terrified that Monty is about to open it and bring forth the wrath of Thor. 'They're the ancient tools that Ma and Pa told me about last night that'll open the "portal to the past" to enable us to travel back in time.'

'I like the sound of that, travelling back in time, but why so nervous about me touching the box?'

'Well if you don't have the gift and say the right words before opening it then you're cursed and it's not pleasant.'

'Whoops,' he replies, quickly dropping it back on the bed as Charity makes her way to the bathroom.

'What's this "portal to the past"?'

'I'll tell you at breakfast when everyone's there.'

'Hurry up then,' yells Monty as he makes his way to the kitchen, while Charity puts her face on and squeezes into her comfortable stretchy black jeans and top.

'Good morning everyone and isn't it a lovely day?' she says chirpily as they all settle down for breakfast while she relays her nightly adventure, culminating in telling them about opening the 'portal to the past' and going back in time. Everyone listens intently as they imagine themselves transported back in time and reliving history.

'It's amazing, you mean we can actually be transported back to nineteen-forty?' shrieks Robyn whose whole body is shaking with excitement, 'but how and when?'

'I'm not sure yet. I must study the *Sacred Book of Angels*, which contains all the legends of the ancient tarot cards and how to use them wisely. Once I know the secret of the power behind the cards of Thor then I'll feel secure in using them to open the universal gateway to the past.'

'That means you've got until next Monday at noon,' says Jack.

'I know, so it's important that I get it right, otherwise we'll have to wait another thousand years and I don't think that's an option.'

'Boy, oh boy, my army days seem dull in comparison to the wonders I've experienced since meeting you and Monty.'

'And they say a driver's life is dull in the servants' quarters,' jokes Aunt Lizzy as she dishes up another round of toast.

'Not in this house, Lizzy, that's for sure,' chips in Robyn as they all laugh and joke together before finishing breakfast and setting off on their separate assignments;

Charity to pick up Sam at the hospital and do a spot of sleuthing; Monty and Jack to use their connections in the Secret Service to discover what dark secrets lie hidden deep in the archives of the government; leaving Robyn with her avalanche of phone calls to make, and Aunt Lizzy to pick the brains of her friends.

'Aren't you ready yet?' Charity jokes as she nimble foots it into the hospital ward to pick up Sam, who's feeling a little sorry for herself as Leo hasn't been in to visit.

'Oh it's you!'

'What do mean, "Oh it's you"? That's a fine welcome for your best friend who's come all this way to take you home.'

'I know, I'm sorry, old girl, but I'm kind of disappointed that Leo didn't come to visit or pick me up.'

'Now stop that, you know he loves you to bits, but he's a High Court judge in the middle of a big case and you've been in one day and a bit and I bet he's been ringing you constantly,' replies Charity as she helps Sam pack her overnight bag.

'Well he is a very important man and it's a very high profile case,' Sam replies, suddenly feeling much better as she touches up her make-up and hair.

'Exactly! Being married to such a prominent man has its downsides occasionally, but you're big enough to handle it,' says Charity, stroking her ego while smiling wryly to herself as she watches Sam preening herself with pride at being married to a man with such a 'high standing in the community'.

While Sam checks out at the reception desk, Charity uses this as an opportunity to ask some questions about the old woman.

'I was chatting to the ward sister the other day when

she mentioned an old woman, Blank Liz, who used to be a regular patient here over the years, but sadly died recently.'

'That's right, old Liz, the bag lady, but why are you interested in her?' the receptionist asks.

'I'm a novelist and one of the characters in my book is a mysterious old woman who lives as a tramp to hide a secret past. It intrigued me that the hospital actually had a homeless old lady as a regular patient and I thought that this would be a perfect opportunity to do some research for my book and was wondering if you could tell me anything more about her.'

'A novelist! How exciting. What's your name? I might have read some of your books,' she replies, suddenly becoming much more helpful.

'It's actually my first book and I'm keen to get things as authentic and accurate as possible so I would be enormously grateful for your help.'

'Well I can't tell you much except that she ended up at the hospital a couple of times each year with the usual complaint of chest infection and malnutrition brought on by the life she led. I don't think she had a regular roof over her head so to speak but always stayed at the Holy Trinity shelter not far from here whenever she was discharged for a couple of days. Father Thomas, the chaplain who runs the shelter, used to take pity on her whenever he visited the hospital doing his "holy rounds" as I like to call them, and always looked after her when she was discharged. If anybody knows anything about her he would be your best bet.'

'Did she have any belongings that might give a clue as to her real identity?'

'She used to carry a large plastic bag around with her but wouldn't let anybody take it from her when she was admitted, and nobody really wanted to look after it anyway as it was a bit smelly and dirty. I guess Father Thomas might know where it is as he was the last one to see her when he was called in to give her the last rites and may have taken it back to the shelter as it wasn't handed in at reception.'

'Thanks a lot, you've been really helpful,' says Charity before continuing, 'where exactly did you say this shelter was?'

'Turn left outside the main entrance and cross over the road. Walk a further two hundred yards until you come across a small alley leading to Bulldog Lane where you'll find the shelter. It's next door to the Holy Trinity chapel where Father Thomas lives.'

'Thanks again,' shouts Charity as she and Sam rush out of the ward.

'What did you say your name was again so that I can buy your book when it comes out?' yells the receptionist after them as they disappear out of sight.

'Here we are, Bulldog Lane,' Charity says as they stand outside the shelter.

'What a dump, who'd want to stay here? It's the pits,' remarks Sam as they stare at what looks like a makeshift hut with a rusty corrugated roof and dirty plastic windows erected next door to an equally shabby and rundown church.

'I must admit it's pretty dingy and depressing,' Charity replies, suddenly feeling incredibly sad for the old woman.

'Can I help you, ladies?'

An incredibly handsome man aged about 40 and at least 6ft tall with dark curly hair, brown eyes and the most dazzling white smile stands at the entrance of the shelter wearing a priest's collar underneath a grey sweatshirt and blue jeans.

'What a dish and what a waste,' whispers Sam underneath her breath to Charity as the two of them stare almost mesmerised at this vision of pulsating manhood standing before them.

'Hi, my name's Sam and this is my friend Charity,' leaps in Sam, flirting like mad before Charity can open her mouth. 'We're doing some research on the homeless and were wondering if you could help us?'

Charity glares, irritated at being pushed aside while Sam continues to flirt outrageously.

'Please come in, my name's Father Thomas and I run this centre with the help of volunteers and the good nuns of the Holy Trinity church.'

They follow him, casting their eyes over his pert bum as he leads them into a small makeshift office, blushing like teenage girls as their stomachs perform somersaults and their hormones suddenly start raging inside them. They both smile at each other, completely taken aback at their instant attraction to this man of the cloth and the inability to control their own emotions. As Sam continues to flirt, Charity pulls herself together, asking, 'While visiting Sam in hospital the other day, I got chatting to the old lady in the bed next to her, who I believe didn't have a name, so was known as Blank Liz, and was sad to hear that she died soon after my last visit. (A small white lie to a priest in this instance wasn't really that wicked Charity thought to herself.) I was interested in finding out more about her as I believe she'll be buried in a pauper's grave and thought it might be nice to have her real name put on her gravestone and understand from the receptionist at the hospital that you may be able to help us.'

'What a kind and generous act, but not one that Liz would've appreciated, I'm sad to say.'

'Oh, why's that then?' Sam asks coyly.

'I'd been giving Liz shelter here for several years but she was an incredibly secretive person and gave very little away and in particular never told anyone her name. Even when I was giving her the last rites and asked her one last time for her name she still wouldn't tell me. She just kept saying over and over again, "I win, I win, they lose, they lose and they'll never find it now".'

'Do you know what she meant by that, Father?' Charity asks.

'I'm afraid not. It's strange, for over the years when she used to stay here, recovering, she'd cry out in her sleep those very same words, and the night duty staff would try and comfort her and often asked her what she meant. But she'd always reply with the same answer, "Can't tell you, can't tell, you're not authorised. Need the code need the code can't tell you without the code".'

'What code?' Charity asks, feeling a sudden surge of excitement as she pictures the old woman as a wartime spy.

'I don't know. She'd never elaborate on any of her strange little comments, which she'd repeat over and over again. You see, no one ever really had a real conversation with her, as she always spoke in riddles. There were two sides to Liz: silence and riddles. She'd either sit in complete silence staring into space rocking back and forth for hours or speak in riddles, but always saying the same things over and over again. As the years went by you just accepted the way she was, giving her the occasional bed for the night and some food and clothes when she needed them. I was probably the closest person to her in the last seven years and yet I knew absolutely nothing about her except that she had a deep fear of intimacy of any kind and didn't have one single friend.'

'Did she have any belongings, Father, that might shed some light on who she was?' they ask simultaneously, which startles him as he begins to suspect that these are no ordinary women.

'Somehow I get the impression that you're both hiding something, and unless you tell me what that is, this conversation's over,' he replies sharply, which only seems to add to his masculine charm.

'It's nothing sinister, Father,' replies Charity, 'it's just that we lead rather dull lives and suddenly listening to you telling us about authorisation and needing codes evokes all sorts of imaginative thoughts in our heads.'

He suddenly relaxes again, laughing aloud. 'Well, ladies, I don't think that poor old Liz had much of a life and certainly I can't imagine her dealing in secret codes, but you're welcome to look through her belongings, which consist of one rather sad plastic bag filled with a few old clothes and trinkets.'

'Thank you, Father,' they both reply as he collects a dirty old black plastic bag from the store cupboard sadly labelled Blank Liz. As he empties the contents onto the floor a tremendous feeling of emptiness and loss sweeps over them as they gaze upon the pitiful items that sum up the life of one old woman. A moth-eaten cardigan and two tatty old skirts wrapped around three pairs of knickers, two bras and some old socks that have seen better days. Folded inside another plastic bag is an old pair of shoes, a threadbare blouse that was once white but now bears the trampled colour of time, and an old vest with more holes than material, tied together with an elastic band. A brown envelope containing four hair slides, a brush and comb, a mirror, and a pair of very old gold earrings that are misshapen, and a locket with a picture of a pretty dark-haired woman aged about 20 inside. It's a very old picture showing the old woman as a beautiful young lady, smiling, which tears at their hearts as they ponder for a few moments upon what she'd become. Charity holds the locket in her hand as she closes her eyes and uses her psychic powers to connect with the old woman's spirit.

'What do you see?' Sam asks, suddenly realising that the spirit of the angels glows within Charity's face as Father Thomas suddenly sees her true soul and marvels in the revelation that appears before him. Her face, glowing brighter and brighter as the gift of 'pure sight' enters her body and the picture of the young girl comes to life within her own soul.

'I see a young, impetuous girl boarding a train with her long dark hair flowing in the wind. She waves goodbye to her family at the station as the train begins its journey. She's full of excitement for a future that promises so much, and yet is sad at leaving her loved ones behind. An innocent in the ways of the world who trusts so easily and loves so completely; she's a child in a woman's body who's on her way to her destiny.'

'What destiny?' Sam asks excitedly, while Father Thomas continues to stare intensely at Charity's face, which suddenly loses its light as the shadow of fear crosses over it.

'Polly, her name is Polly and she's travelling towards her new life, which is full of promises and yet there's darkness just around the corner waiting for her.'

The vision disappears as Charity clings to the locket, feeling wretched inside as tears flow down her face.

'What happened? Are you OK?' Sam yells as she grabs Charity's hand.

'I'm fine, Sam, I couldn't hold onto her but I'm sure it was the old woman.'

'Who are you really and why are you interested in Liz?' the father asks as he tries to understand, for even though he's chosen to follow the Lord he's never actually felt a 'connection' until he saw the light in Charity's face.

'I'm Charity Holmes, the Inceptor, and Polly, the old woman, visited me in spirit, seeking my help.'

'An inceptor, I've read about people like you in the scriptures. You have the power of "sight" otherwise known as "Clear Seeing" and can communicate with the spirits. It's written that inceptors have the power of the angels within them and can see into the past and future and have the power to cross over into the spirit world. But why has the spirit of Liz asked for your help?'

'Her name and life were stolen from her in the mortal world and she wants them back so that she can rest in peace, and I've been charged with that quest and must help her before it's too late.'

'What do you mean too late?' he asks.

'I've only got until **15th August** when judgement will be passed and her destiny in the spirit world will be decided so you see, Father, I really do want to help her.'

He smiles, looking deep into her eyes and for a moment their souls become as one as they feel complete in their desire to help Polly, the old woman, who at last has a name.

'Take the locket, Charity, you may need it again.'

'Thank you, Father, and the Lord be with you always,' she says softly, placing the locket in her bag before taking Sam home.

'Will you be OK on your own, for I must return and read the *Sacred Book of Angels* if we're to enter the portal on Monday?' Charity enquires as she helps Sam unpack.

'Don't worry about me, old girl, I'm fine. You get off home. Leo will be back soon and we've got loads to catch up on.'

'Boy, I'm ready for this, thanks, Lizzy,' Charity sighs, settling into her big soft leather armchair in her quiet room as Aunt Lizzy serves up tea.

'How's Sam, darling?'

'Just fine, Lizzy, I've dropped her home, and Leo will take care of her. Have you heard from the others?'

'Not yet, darling, but you know the lads, come dinner time they'll soon find their way home.'

'We'll chat later about the day, Lizzy, when everyone's together. I need to do a spot of reading now,' says Charity as Aunt Lizzy closes the door behind her.

Charity finishes her tea and then carefully opens the *Sacred Book of Angels* as she settles back to read the secrets of the god Thor.

6

Portal to the Past

While Charity turns the dusty yellow parchment pages that creak with the sound of a thousand years of knowledge handed down through generations of inceptors, she can hear the distant voices of the angels singing within this ancient tarot bible. Legend has it that the pages are bound together with the skin of serpents and painted in their blood (symbolising immortalisation by the shedding of their skin), enabling them to travel through the vortex of universal time. Carved into the book cover are two serpents forming a circle inside which is the Angel of Enlightenment, protected by the four creatures of Ezekiel, who guard the circle. **Man** represents the mortality of human life. The **ox** represents the burden of man's sins. The **lion** represents inner strength. Finally, the **eagle** represents victory to those with a pure soul. For only those who are pure of heart can turn the pages and know the secrets held within the *Sacred Book of Angels*.

Finally she comes to the page that shows the secrets of Thor and the power of his ancient tarot cards, which will enable her to travel back to the time of war. There are six cards depicting the mind and soul of Thor. They are laid out in the order that must be used by the inceptor to evoke the 'power of infinite sight', which will open the portal to the past. Once Charity lays the cards out and uses her power of 'Clear Seeing' to open her mind's eye to the Universal Unconscious then the gateway to the past is hers to control.

. The **six** cards must be placed clockwise and face up on a round table forming an impenetrable ring, with card number **one** placed in the centre representing the power of the inceptor. The other cards represent **five** people whose souls are bound together with the inceptor's forming one pure light of golden energy. All **six** must travel through the portal with the cards or they'll not be able to open it again at the other side when they need to return twelve hours later.

Card one	The Body	**The Inceptor**	Holds the power of mind and soul
Card two	The Inquirer	**The maze**	Searching for the way through
Card three	The Raven	**Flight/danger**	Fly through time at your own risk
Card four	The Stars	**'Eight' stars**	Opening/closing of gateway to the past
Card five	The Voyage	**The ship**	The voyage of time begins
Card six	The Mirror	**Reflection of time**	The past turns full circle

On the next page, written in the ancient tongue of Thor (which only an inceptor of the highest level is able to decipher) are the words to be spoken by Charity to evoke his power and open the portal. As she looks at the cards again Destiny calls to her, for those who form the impenetrable ring are brought together through blood, friendship, love and trust to become one powerful force; the very same RING that is her family: Monty, Robyn, Aunt Lizzy, Sam and Jack. Now she knows what to do and sees the power behind each card.

Card one	The Inceptor	=	**Charity**	=	The power of the angels
Card two	The Inquirer	=	**Monty**	=	The power of absolute love
Card three	The Raven	=	**Jack**	=	Protection of the soldier of war
Card four	The Stars	=	**Robyn**	=	The fearlessness of youth
Card five	The Voyage	=	**Aunt Lizzy**	=	The power of family
Card six	The Mirror	=	**Sam**	=	The strength of true friendship

Just as she turns the last page, the angels whisper the warning that must be listened to. 'All that open the portal and travel through the timeless gateway to the past must return. Break the power of the RING and the "past is your future".'

The shadow of fear crosses her heart as she listens to the voices of her guardians, knowing that they must all return together or be lost forever in the past. How can she ask this of her family, to risk their future to save one soul? Just at that moment the door opens and she hears the laughter of Monty and Jack as Aunt Lizzy tells them off for disturbing her when the sign outside says 'Quiet Time'.

'Sorry, Spud, forgot about the sign.' Monty rushes in, eager to tell her his news, kissing her passionately on the lips as she closes the book that foretells their destiny.

'I hope you've worked out how to open this magical gateway to the past as Jack and I have uncovered a top secret file marked "**Operation Fish**", which involved the British War Cabinet, Royal Navy and Canadian government, plus...'

'None other than the prime minister and First Lord of the Admiralty, Churchill,' Jack interrupts excitedly, finishing Monty's sentence and stealing his moment of glory.

'Thank you, Jack,' growls Monty, glaring crossly at him

'Well I've got some interesting gossip myself, which I didn't believe until now,' says Aunt Lizzy excitedly.

'What gossip?' asks Monty, all ears.

'Well apparently it involves the Bank of England, Bank of Canada and the Sun Life Assurance building in Montreal, Canada.'

'Hold it there, people,' interrupts Charity as she suddenly realises that it won't be a question of asking them if they want to travel back in time, but how to stop them.

'Let's all go into the lounge and wait for Robyn before we say any more, for I've got some news as well and I need to have everyone together before any more decisions are made.'

'What news and what about Sam?' Monty asks, sensing that Charity seems worried and not her usual inquisitive self.

'We'll ring her and put the phone on speaker so we can share our news together and then make the necessary decision,' replies Charity as she leads the way to the lounge with Monty, Jack and Aunt Lizzy following behind, suddenly feeling that cold shiver of fear run through them.

'Well you lot look glum. What's up?' Robyn asks as she bundles in carrying a thick file of paperwork under her arm.

'Charity's being serious and won't say anything until we're all together,' replies Monty as he helps himself to a drink.

'Ooh, ah, that sounds mysterious, but where's Sam?'

'At home, but we can get her on speaker,' replies Jack as he dials her number.

'Hi, Sam, Jack here, how's things?'

'Never better, Jack, what's up at your end?'

'It's conference time and you're on speaker.'

'Hold on a sec then, I'd better sort the phone out and make myself comfortable,' she replies, switching her phone to speaker before shouting to Leo, who's in the bathroom, to join her.

'No need to yell the house down, love, I'm not deaf yet.'

'Sorry, Petal, but the RING is in conference and may need your advice.'

'I'm very expensive,' he jokes, stroking his thick hair, which he's very proud of as most men his age are losing theirs. He's even more vain than Sam, always checking his reflection in the mirror and watching his diet so he doesn't look portly. But underneath all that vanity he's a kind and generous man with a sharp wit and brilliant mind who adores his much younger wife and would do anything for her.

'Hi, everyone, what's so important that it can't wait?' he asks, cosying up against Sam on the couch with drinks in hand.

'Great to hear your voice again, Leo, it's been a while.'

'Good to hear from you too, Charity.'

'Well let's begin.'

Charity relays her day, the details of culminating in telling them that should they choose to help her open the portal then they risk being left in the past should one of them not make it back to complete the RING.

'I don't like the sound of not making it back, my darling,' says Aunt Lizzy, frowning as Robyn quickly puts her two pennies worth in:

'Of course, it's a risk, but look at the golden opportunity before us to travel back in time and experience history in the making, how can we not go?'

'I agree, we must open the portal,' Monty says anxiously. 'To go back when Churchill was prime minister and Britain was on the verge of war – I can't believe we're contemplating not going.'

Jack leaps in: 'We must go: there are secrets about the war and Churchill, which have remained hidden for the last sixty years that we could unlock. I agree with Monty and Robyn – it's worth the risk.'

'Absolutely,' yells Sam down the speaker as Leo interrupts.

'Just a second here, don't I have a say? You're my wife and I'm not in this so-called "Ring of Power" so if something goes wrong we'll never see each other again.'

Sam holds his hand, realising how selfish she sounded in not considering his feelings.

'Of course you have a say, Petal, and the thought of us being apart in two separate times is abhorrent, but I must do this, for if I don't complete the RING the portal can't be opened. It was meant to be, destiny has called upon the RING again, and we must answer it.'

Leo squeezes her hand as he looks into her face knowing that if he holds her back he loses his beautiful wife anyway, for she is a fearless spirit who can't be caged, so to keep her, he must let her fly free.

'Well that just leaves you, Spud,' says Monty quietly as he waits in trepidation for her answer. For although he's fearful he knows that deep down she won't be able to resist the chance to save Polly, plus if anything does go wrong, at least they'll still be together even if it is in another time. Sometimes he can be ruthless in his determination to seek the truth even if it means risking everything.

Charity remains silent as she battles with her conscience, worried for her loved ones yet, as Monty silently predicts in his heart, unable to resist the call of destiny.

'I'm worried about Lizzy and Leo, for if they're unhappy then we can't ignore their feelings,' she replies, wrestling with her desire to do right by all.

'Don't fret about me, my darling, I may be scared, but I'm a Merrick and you know our motto, "Feel the fear and then go beyond", so I'm with the RING,' Aunt Lizzy replies, anxious that her beloved Charity knows she's always behind her whatever decision she makes.

'I love Sam more than my own life, but I also love her free spirit and fearless loyalty for her friends so I know that she must do this,' says Leo softly, while Sam smiles proudly. She has the love of a good and honourable man, whose love for her is more selfless than hers, as deep within her own soul she's not so sure that if it were he seeking to travel through the portal that she would be so willing to let him go.

'That's it, we're all agreed, the portal will be opened at noon on Monday, and God be with us all,' Charity announces as she sits up straight looking around the room at her beloved family, secretly hoping that she's made the right decision.

'Amen to that,' replies Aunt Lizzy, making her usual sign of the cross when danger lurks around the corner. Monty, Jack and Robyn breathe a sigh of relief at getting closer to their dream of reliving history.

'Well now that we've got the serious business out of the way, let's gather information and see where we're at,' say Charity assertively as she puts her worries about Monday and the portal to one side.

'You mentioned something about a top secret file hidden in the archives, honey?' she looks at Monty, knowing that he can't wait to spill the beans on his discovery.

'Hidden! That's an understatement. Jack and I had to call in some heavy duty favours to dig up this file, and believe me, Spud, it's dynamite.' His body shakes with excitement at what they've both uncovered.

'Well don't keep us in suspense, go on, go on,' Robyn interrupts, eager to know all, as she dumps the file on the coffee table, making herself comfortable on the couch next to Charity. Jack hands her her favourite drink.

'The file is merely a skeleton of information, as "**Operation Fish**" was so secret that few contemporary references exist. Very little was committed to paper and the handful of people who organised it did it nearly all by word of mouth. There were no official communiqués, and vital decisions affecting the future of Britain were often, according to our source, scribbled on scraps of paper. The instigator of this secret operation was Churchill himself. In late May 1940, when France was teetering on the brink of military defeat, and Britain was left to fight Hitler's invading army on its own, he called the War Cabinet into a secret session to discuss plans for shipping the vast stocks of gold stored in the vaults of the Bank of England in Threadneedle Street to Canada. Even more crucial was his decision to evacuate all the negotiable securities held by private citizens and business organisations across the U-boat infested Atlantic to a top secret location in Montreal. When you add both the gold and securities together they represented almost the entire wealth of Britain. It was a last-ditch survival plan by Churchill because if the Germans did invade and the gold and securities fell into their hands Britain would be finished as it wouldn't be able to buy dollars. Without dollars Britain couldn't buy weapons and materials of war from the only available source – the United States. It was a desperate gamble by Churchill, which, if it had failed, would have brought about a disaster of such magnitude that Britain would have been forced to sue for peace.'

'I can't believe what I'm hearing,' says Robyn. 'You're saying that Churchill, one of this country's greatest prime ministers, devised, orchestrated and then instigated the removal of Britain's entire wealth across the Atlantic to another country, in collusion with the War Cabinet, Bank of England and government officials and the Royal Navy

70

without the people of this nation being aware of what was happening effectively to "their money".'

'I know. It shook Jack and me up, and in our business you tend to be somewhat shock proof, but it's true. Effectively five hundred million pounds worth of gold, at 1940 values, and seventy tons of securities, worth a sum that can only be estimated, were shipped in lots of between one million and ten million pounds in over a hundred merchant ships from the UK to Canada and then on to the USA in 1940. It would appear that survival in modern warfare has more to do with economics than strategy,' replies Monty, still getting his head around the notion that even great prime ministers like Churchill have hidden skeletons, which when dug up can still evoke passions some 60 odd years later.

'That connects with what I've heard today, my darlings,' pipes in Aunt Lizzy, who's keen to add her bit of knowledge to the pot of intrigue that's beginning to brew into a very hot soup.

'You said something about Bank of England and Canada plus an Insurance building?' Jack asks, intrigued at how she's managed to uncover information that's linked to a top secret file that's been hidden for over 60 years.

'That's right, my darling, I was chatting with old Mr Parr's housekeeper, Brenda, over lunch and asked her if she new anything about his past as he'd be about the same age as Polly our old woman. She said that he often rambled on about when he was a young bank clerk working at the Bank of England during 1940 when the Securities Manager at the bank, a Roland Uppingham, asked him to do some checking on the Bank of Canada. He thought it odd at the time because he was summoned to a room in an office away from the bank in which two other men in dark suits sat quietly in the corner, listening to Mr Uppingham giving him his instructions. He was

71

told to not write anything down and to only report back to him with the specific information that he was required to get, which he had to memorise. He had to ask the Bank of Canada to assist in finding a building that was suitable to hold securities with two main requirements. **One**, it had to have a fifty by sixty foot burglar proof vault with eight thousand square feet of working space. **Two**, it must be in an absolutely secure location. They came back with just one building that fitted these requirements: the workshops at the Sun Life Assurance headquarters, which were deep down in the solid rock of the Island of Montreal. Once he had done all of that he suddenly received a promotion and was moved to another bank, but not before agreeing to say nothing about his meeting, the two other men and his discussions with the Bank of Canada. He told Brenda that it was because he did exactly what he was told and never mentioned it again to anybody that his career rocketed until he became president of an International bank here in London until he retired eighteen years ago aged sixty-five.'

'Wow, who needs to work in the Secret Service when you can get all the information via the housekeepers' gossip network,' Robyn jokes.

'We all have our uses, my darling,' replies Aunt Lizzy, feeling very pleased with herself.

'It's clear that destiny has crossed Polly's path with mine, as she was waiting for me, and finally her patience was rewarded when I visited Sam in hospital. In death she called to me and knew that I would follow her trail from the hospital to Father Thomas and that I'd find her locket and see the beginning of her journey. In spirit she knew that Monty and Jack would uncover the secret file once I accepted her quest and that Lizzy was friendly with old Mr Parr's housekeeper and his past, albeit in a tenuous way, would form a link to hers. There are no coincidences here, family, everything was meant to be and I see now that we have no choice. It's no accident that I'm the custodian of the *Sacred Book of Angels*, which together with the power of the cards of Thor forms the RING that'll open the portal to the past. Again our future has been foretold. The past has become our present and it is into the past that we must journey.'

The room is filled with silence as they listen to Charity's words, and once again it dawns on them that their choices somehow always seem predestined.

'Here I am thinking that I'm in control of my life and making my own choices and decisions only to hear that actually my thoughts are already somebody else's and that I'm merely a puppet to be used by the spirits to do their bidding,' says Monty angrily.

'You're no puppet, honey, none of us are. We all have free choice and can choose to help Polly or not. The spirits don't control your mind, you do. All I'm saying is that life has many different paths that we can choose to go down at any time, but inevitably all these paths will lead to the same end; like a pyramid, all corners come to the same point. We all made the decision to help Polly and open the portal together so, yes, destiny comes a calling, but we ultimately have the choice in how to answer it.'

'All I know is that I've been given the chance to open the gateway to the past and relive history and I for one want to leap through it. That's the only path I'd have chosen, no matter how many lay before me. I choose the path to the past,' says Robyn so assertively that she almost knocks her drink over as she thumps it down on the table.

'OK, OK, that's settled then, everyone here is in control and we choose the paths we walk down, maybe!' Jack says jokingly, trying to make light of their inner fears before asking Robyn, 'What's all that paperwork you're carrying, anything interesting?'

'You bet, and again, dare I say! Yet another coincidence in that when checking all the hostels, and might I add there were hundreds of them, I found an interesting link between our old woman, Polly, and a now defunct employment agency called Bright Services, who specialised in providing live-in maids and gentleman butlers to the well-heeled. Tracking back through all the hostels and homeless shelters over the years I finally discovered the name of a woman called Polly Melrose. Coincidence number **one**. The same name it now transpires as our old woman, who signed on for state benefit briefly in 1965 when she was forty-five, which would make her the same age as our old woman. Coincidence number **two**. I then managed to get hold of her records, using let's say slightly dubious methods that I won't go into, and discovered that she signed on at this agency when she was twenty years old and secured a position as a housemaid for a family called the Uppinghams in May 1940. Coincidence number **three**. **One**, **two**, **three**, the TIE is linked. Unfortunately that's where the paper trail ends, as I can't find any formal records of the Bright Services agency, her contract or where she came from and how she got the job. Polly only collected state benefit for a couple of months before "disappearing" through the system until now.'

'What about the Uppinghams, did you find anything out about them?' interrupts Leo, who by now is completely immersed in the life of Polly Melrose as it's not often he's privy to the RING's meetings and is just beginning to realise what an exciting yet dangerous life Sam and the RING lead compared to his relatively staid life as a judge. He indulges his beautiful wife with what he perceives as her hobby, playing at detective, but now for the first time the reality of her life dawns on him. The RING is the vital key between the spirit and mortal world, which, when turned, opens the doorway to limitless wonders. The adrenalin begins to pump through his veins and his heart starts racing as he experiences, for the first time, the addictive elixir of entering the world of spirits.

'I'm afraid the information about Bright Services and its clients is incomplete in that everything was destroyed by fire in **August 1945**, the second date given to Charity by the Angel of Judgement. Coincidence number **four**. Official records state that Bright Services offices were burned to the ground by an unknown arsonist's attack, destroying all their records and it seems their existence as well. I only found this information out from the Social Services form that Polly filled in when she claimed benefit and had to declare when she was last in employment. I tried to trace the family tree of the Uppinghams at Company House, but strangely there doesn't appear to be any record of them ever existing. Yet here we have an account by Mr Parr's housekeeper that he worked for a Mr Uppingham in 1940 and a documented note in a Social Services file that a Polly Melrose worked for them. How can an entire family and business disappear without trace?'

'Very easily,' Monty replies as Jack nods in agreement with that wry smile on his face.

'What do you mean very easily?' Charity asks.

'One's life is made up of paper, bits of paper that record your existence. Destroy the paper and your existence is no more. Somewhere someone very high up went to great lengths to wipe out the existence of Polly Melrose, Ronald Uppingham and the Bright Services agency. They almost succeeded until Polly signed on for social security and somehow that piece of paper remained intact.'

'It could be that the person who instigated the fire and paper trail destruction is now dead, and when Polly signed on briefly all those years ago it was missed,' interrupts Jack, keen to add his two pennies worth.

'Good point, Jack, but that means their identity probably died with them and also the link to the past,' replies Monty.

'Not necessarily so, honey,' Charity replies, smiling. 'We have the portal to the past.'

7

The Innocent

It's Monday, the first day of the eighth month as the RING gathers in the garden of 29 Chalfont Square to invoke the power of Thor and open the portal to the past. There's a chill in the air, which carries the sound of ancient whispers as darkness overtakes the light of day. The clouds join forces to eclipse the heavens and bring forth the timeless gateway to the past. The round table stands before them as Charity places the cards of Thor clockwise in front of their respective 'souls of pure energy' in the order that is written in the *Sacred Book of Angels* and so begins the impenetrable RING of blood, friendship, love and trust that'll unleash the power of Thor.

Card **one**: Charity, the Inceptor who'll unleash the power of the angels. Card **two**: Monty, the Inquirer, who has the power of absolute love. Card **three**: Jack, the Raven, who brings the power of protection. Card **four**: Robyn, the Stars, who possesses the fearlessness of youth. Card **five**: Aunt Lizzy, the Voyage, who brings the power of family (blood). And finally, card **six**: the Mirror, Sam who brings the strength of true friendship. Leo stands in the shadows, fearful for her and his friends, yet envious of the journey that lies before them. Although he's not part of this ancient RING he has their fate in his hands, which, if he fails, will lock them in the past for ever.

When the portal is opened and the hand of time reaches the eighth minute, he must gather the cards of Thor while placing them in their box and throw them through the portal to Charity as she, the Inceptor, is the last to pass through this timeless gateway. She must not take the cards with her for to do so would break the Ring of Power before she completes the ancient tongue of Thor. He must not fail, for to do so would make the past their future and his beautiful wife would be lost to him for ever. Charity, in her final moments before invoking the power of Thor, hands him the *Sacred Book of Angels*, charging him as its protector until their return.

The time has come and as the clock strikes noon, Charity recites the ancient tongue of Thor.

'Rosoth, God of magic, Tureth, God of timelessness, Gerah, guardian of the gateway, rise up great gods and open the portal, bringing forth the past.' Charity repeats the words three times: 'Rosoth, Tureth, Gerah, rise up and open the portal, bringing forth the past.'

As she recites these ancient words the skies above bring forth the lightning power of the gods through the black clouds of timeless space, as the winds scream the power of Thor through the spirits of the gods. The heavens turn black and the thunder rages as the gods awake from their sleep of a thousand years to invoke their power and rip the skies apart until the blackest of voids appear. The clouds transform into monstrous reflections of the three gods: Rosoth, Tureth and Gerah with their timeless faces depicting the wisdom and power of endless eternity. The void becomes bigger as the angels appear from within the clouds to carry their charges through it and into the chasm of time. Beautiful golden-winged angels of pure translucent light that fly like twinkling stars towards the circle of light that beams up towards the heavens from the **six** that form the Ring of Power. They float above their charges, six

78

angels for six mortals, each with the sword of Thor in their right hand to ward off evil spirits that might cling to their charges and travel with them into the void in the hope of rebirth into another time. With their left hand they lift their charges up from within the light of the RING and carry them towards the portal as they wield their swords of Thor in the air so no evil can touch them. One by one the RING disappears through the portal until only Charity remains, as she looks at Leo with trust in her eyes, while her angel lifts her into the air, flying towards the portal. He rushes to the table as the clock strikes the eighth minute and the portal begins to close, leaving just 60 seconds for him to gather the cards of Thor. Desperately he fights the clock while he gathers each card anticlockwise from number **six** to **one** as the pure light of the ring begins to fade and the power of the cards of Thor diminishes until the RING is broken. Then just at the final second before the eighth minute has struck, he closes the box. For a moment he senses something cold around his hand. Looking up into the skies to see Charity with her hands stretched out ready to catch it, he raises his arm high and with one powerful thrust throws it to her. His prayers are answered as she smiles at him, carrying the box in her arms as the portal closes behind her and the past becomes the present.

They're carried protectively through this seemingly endless dark swirling tunnel of space by their golden angels as the past briefly flashes before them, showing snapshots of the darkness of war. They see the destruction of the towers in New York on that fateful day and the horrors of civil war in Northern Ireland, plus the pitiful dead bodies of children in the Vietnam War. They see the bombing of Pearl Harbor until suddenly their golden angels gently place them in a dark, damp, cold room that appears to be moving underneath them before they disappear back into the void as the portal closes and their future becomes the past.

'Where are we and how do we know that we're in 1940?' Robyn asks, suddenly losing her fearlessness of youth for a second.

'I think we're in a ship,' replies Jack as their eyes adjust to the darkness and they see endless rows of large wooden crates stacked high all around them. They feel the room sway and see beams of light filter through round holes as they slowly manoeuvre their way through the hundreds of crates crammed tightly together.

'Look, the door over there, it's got writing on it,' shouts Sam as they read the white painted words: 'Danger – Ammunition Locker'.

'My god, we're in a battleship,' shrieks Sam as they all stand totally still, suddenly realising that they've been transported onto a battleship in the middle of the Atlantic.

'Check this out,' says Monty excitedly as he examines one of the boxes more closely.

'HMS *Emperor* – Despatch – Greenock **21.06 1940**.'

'They're guns, we're surrounded by guns,' screeches Sam, suddenly wishing that she was back home in the safe arms of her beloved Leo.

'No they're not,' replies Monty as he notices a split in one of the crates and can see something golden shimmering through the crack. 'It's gold bullion!' he cries loudly. 'We're in a battleship carrying what must be billions of pounds worth of gold bullion.'

'Plus securities,' interrupts Jack as he pushes his hand through a rather large crack in the crate and pulls out a £100 bond.

'Glory be to God, it's all true, they really did take all the money out of Britain and transport it to Canada,' Aunt Lizzy says in astonishment, making her usual sign of the cross.

80

'I know, great isn't it,' shrieks Robyn excitedly before asking Charity, 'How did you manage to get the portal to transport us to this ship in the right time zone.'

'As I placed the cards of Thor on the table and began reciting his words, my third eye saw the time and place where I wished to go and carried my vision to the gods who sent the angels to guide us.'

'You never cease to amaze me, Spud,' says Monty proudly as he looks lovingly at his beautiful wife.

'Why transport us back to this ship and time?' Jack asks, intrigued at being placed aboard a battleship in the middle of the war where they could be blown to smithereens any minute.

Everyone suddenly looks at Charity as it dawns on them that it's hardly the safest of places she could have chosen for their trip back into the past.

'Because whatever happened to change Polly's destiny, it started here on this ship and was the catalyst that began the chain of events, which would ultimately lead to her "invisible life". We have only twelve hours to discover the evil that was perpetrated aboard this ship and which finally came to an end on **15th August 1945**. This is the first ship of many that would travel across the waters to Canada, but it's aboard this ship that dark deeds were planned and instigated by evil and greedy people, which ultimately led to the death of an innocent.'

'What innocent?' Sam asks.

'I don't know yet but in the Court of Past Souls Polly said that the twin brother had a "murderous heart" and that they "stole the life of another innocent" in the name of greed. Well I've met the brother and his heart beats within a dark soul, which my gift tells me was given over to Lucifer when his greed led to the most heinous crime of all – murder.'

'Murder, whose murder?' asks Sam, now totally enthralled.

'That's why we're here,' she replies. 'With a ship full of gold, envy, greed and treachery will soon fester and grow in the dark side of a man's soul until the demon lord Lucifer comes calling with promises of great riches in return for the soul of an innocent.'

'But the brother died young,' Monty remarks, looking puzzled.

'Exactly, honey, something went horribly wrong, which resulted in his death along with the "innocent". Remember the twin sister said that Polly betrayed him and then condemned his soul to hell, so whatever his treacherous plans were she destroyed them, but not before he stole the life of an innocent. I think he betrayed her love and she in turn betrayed his plans for the future by stealing what he coveted, which ultimately led to his death and the destruction of not only Polly's life but that of his family as well.'

'If it all happened on this ship why did it take five years to end in 1945?' Robyn asks, by now totally confused.

'Again I'm not sure, but let's surmise that the plan was to steal some gold and securities, hide them and then wait the war out, which coming from the future we know lasted until 1945, but the plan went wrong and the brother dies leaving his conspirators searching for the stolen gold.'

'Ah ha, and Polly knew where it was, but she disappeared,' Sam replies, attempting to sound extremely intelligent.

'Precisely, you remember her words, "They want what I know but I was too clever for them and made myself invisible and they'll never find it now. I win, I win, they lose, they lose."'

Suddenly there are voices at the door as they rush to hide behind crates filled with billions of pounds worth of gold bullion.

'We shouldn't be in here. We haven't got clearance. I'll lose my job if we get caught.'

'Don't worry, my father's the one who's really in charge of the operation. Your boss is merely the mule carrying the goods.'

A girl giggles shyly as a thin man with a shallow face and wispy greased-backed hair runs his hands all over her body while whispering words of lustful desire in her ear. His voice has a detachment and arrogance about it that Charity recognises immediately.

'It's the twin brother,' she whispers as the RING see a plain, plump girl aged about 22 with a pale face scarred with acne and almost completely masked by black thick-rimmed glasses. Her mousy brown hair is heavily sprayed to keep her 1940s perm in place. She's behaving like a love-struck teenager as she crumbles in his greasy arms, completely spellbound by his every lecherous and, to the onlooker, dishonest words of proclaimed love and desire. His hands are everywhere as she closes her eyes and dreams of a life with her man. His are wide open and looking upon the only object of his desires, the crates of gold, which makes the RING feel pungent with anger as they watch him smirk and smile with envy and greed at what he hopes will soon be his.

'Stop, stop, my love, before someone comes in,' she protests, somewhat weakly as they readjust their clothes.

'You worry too much, Petal, the old goat is snoring away after downing another bottle of whisky and everyone else is too busy fighting the war to care about what we're doing.'

'Sometimes you can be really callous, Harold. The General's a wonderful man who's seen and experienced the destruction and death that the horrors of war bring and tries to escape from the demons that enter his dreams at night and torment him with nightmarish visions by taking the odd glass of whisky to help him sleep.'

This is a woman with a gentle and pure heart who's

desperate for approval and love, which Harold will use and discard without conscience in his desire to acquire the only real object of his dark heart, money and power.

'You're far too soft, Petal, my father's got the measure of General Winkner, he's a drunk, weak man with no backbone. Father says that if we relied on him to win the war then we might as well surrender now as all he's fit for is captaining a ship carrying the weapons of war as no one in the War Cabinet would actually give him command of a real battleship.'

'Your father, your father, sometimes I get tired of hearing how good your father is at everything and how weak everyone else is,' she snaps back sharply.

'Huh, and of course you would know all about bravery and backbone, my little wallflower.'

She cowers in the corner of one of the crates trying to hold back the tears while he callously reminds her of her inadequacies and how fortunate she is to have his 'love'.

'I didn't mean it like that, Harold, please don't be angry with me, you know how much I love you.' she pleads, clinging to his arm as he cleverly torments her with that superior air of detachment and heartlessness that only a man with a dark and evil soul would do to such a fragile and lonely creature.

'What a pig, I'd like to ram that sick smile of his right down his throat, while kneeing him in the balls at the same time,' whispers Robyn, desperately trying to hold back her anger, while watching him manipulate this gentle and frightened girl who would walk on water for this cad.

'How can she not see what a creep he is?' hisses Sam as she nods in agreement with Robyn. Monty and Jack grin at the way all the girls immediately want to string up this Harold from a very high tree.

84

'Prove it!' he replies coldly, his voice withholding the one thing she so desperately seeks from him: his love.

'I can't, you know I can't, how can you ask me to betray the General and the prime minister. All this gold is being used to buy weapons to protect Britain and all our brave soldiers who are fighting the evil that wants to take our liberty.'

He suddenly realises that he's pushing her away with his heartless words and must redeem himself quickly if he's to obtain his true desires.

'Now, now, Elsie my little petal, my own little flower, you know I love you and that I want us to be together for ever but we need money to achieve our dreams,' he replies, wrapping her in his treacherous arms.

'Someone get me a sick bag before I throw up,' Robyn remarks as they all watch the clever manipulation of the gentle Elsie by the detestable Harold.

'But your father's got money and you have a good position that he secured for you at the bank, which together with our love for each other is more than enough to achieve our dreams, Harold, my darling.'

'You are right, my sweet, but I don't want to spend the next twenty-five years trapped at a desk like my father, I'm worth more than that. I want us to have everything, I don't want us to struggle for years when, with just a little clever planning, we can have all our dreams fulfilled. I'm not asking you to betray your country, just help us to have enough money to begin our future together. After all, there are billions of pounds worth of gold and securities on this ship and all I'm asking for is just two million of it, which is a drop in the ocean in comparison to what is actually here, but would secure our future together for ever. Think about it, Petal, it's nothing to them but everything to us.'

'The rat, stealing money that's going to buy weapons

for our brave soldiers, I'm not a violent woman, my darlings, but I'd happily put a bayonet through his cold heart,' snarls Aunt Lizzy as Charity's gift is telling her that this is the 'innocent' that will be destroyed once the evil Harold gets his way and there's nothing she can do about it. They're just observers in the gateway of time who must not disturb its delicate balance, for even the smallest ripple of change in the history of time can cause a tidal wave of destruction in the future.

'Are you sure, Harold? Two million is a lot of money, and our brave soldiers need those weapons.'

The RING watches helplessly, knowing that they can do nothing as she begins to succumb to his evil plot.

'I'm positive, my love,' he replies greasily, before continuing. 'If it was just a few million then I wouldn't even entertain the idea of helping ourselves, but we're talking about billions here, my Petal, more than enough to help our valiant soldiers in war. You know that I wanted to join up myself but was turned down for medical reasons and now all I desire is a secure future for us and our children.'

'When you put it like that, Harold, I suppose we're not actually harming anyone.'

They stand holding each other tightly with his traitorous arms around her as she smiles contentedly to herself. He grins that evil smirk of victory as the RING look on sadly, knowing that her idyllic vision of their future together will soon be shattered by his treachery.

'You know what to do, my Petal, all I need is a copy of the list of securities and their corresponding account numbers held in the General's safe, and remember I'm only interested in the bonds, not the gold.'

'Why just the paper money, Harold, wouldn't it be easier to sell the gold?'

He laughs in that icy superior way of his as he explains. 'Because paper money is so much more flexible than gold, which is bulky and a lot harder to hide, my Petal, whereas when I'm working at the Sun Life building and have the relevant account numbers to go with the bonds I can easily begin the process of creative accounting.'

'What exactly is creative accounting?'

'Oh, my little wallflower, you are a true innocent (the word sends a chill through Charity's body) in the ways of the business world,' he replies as he proceeds to describe his evil plan to her.

'Over a period of several months I will set up a labyrinth of bogus accounts in different names in other banks in Switzerland into which I will gradually transfer two million pounds worth of bonds.'

'But I still don't understand. If you have the account numbers with you at the bank then you don't need to see them now,' she replies, suddenly beginning to feel suspicious about her lover's real intentions towards her.

His earlier opinion of this 'stupid little wallflower' suddenly changes as he begins to realise that she's somewhat smarter than he originally anticipated. They had first met months earlier at his father's house. His father, Roland Uppingham, Securities Manager at the Bank of England, was meeting General Winkner along with members of Churchill's War Cabinet and other bank officials in a secret liaison to discuss the beginning of the evacuation of Britain's wealth to Canada. Harold and Elsie had glanced at each other briefly in the hallway as she accompanied the General in her role as his personal assistant (his alcohol problem meant that his mind tended to wander). Harold wasn't privy to the meeting but immediately realised its significance when his father made it clear to him and his twin sister, Hilary, later that night that they must never reveal to anyone who the visitors were that came to the house that evening. He recognised instantly that the General's assistant would be the key to his plan to steal £2 million from the bank's gold and securities hidden amongst the weapons carried aboard the battleship, HMS *Emperor* on 21st June 1940, and so duly set about seducing her.

'Once the list with accounts numbers is handed over to my superiors in Canada I won't be able to change anything without them noticing, but if I can obtain the list before the ship docks then I can add some bogus accounts in a random pattern crediting them with monies from the bonds, which will only be identifiable to me. The auditors don't check the accounts until the end of the financial year, which is March so that leaves me several months to transfer the two million pounds into the accounts I've set up before anyone notices.'

He feels very pleased with himself until he catches the look on her face, realising that she's suddenly woken up to the fact that he needs her to get to the list in the General's safe. He quickly grabs her in his arms, whispering in her ear, 'Remember, my love, we need each other, for without each other we're nothing. We were meant to meet at my father's house as destiny has brought us together. I love you and if you love me you'll help me so that I can create a safe future for our children and us. I love you, just remember that, my Petal, I love you.'

He repeats the words over and over again as he caresses her body until she's intoxicated by his love and her mind is only full of thoughts of them and their future together. The RING look on as they see this gentle girl cruelly manipulated by this evil man, knowing that once he has his way his need for her will be no more.

'I'll have to wait until I'm sure the General's in one of his deep sleeps, which won't be for another couple of hours when he's had a few more drinks and I can unlock the safe without disturbing him.'

He smiles that smug smirk of victory as she buttons

up her blouse and fixes her hair and make-up while he stands there dreaming of the £2 million that'll soon be his. They agree to meet up in her room later that evening as they close the door behind them, leaving the RING to ponder in silence as it's clear to them that they've just watched the 'innocent' being led to her death.

'What do we do now?' Robyn pleads. 'She's going to die, I know he's going to kill her once she's given him the information. I mean, he can't let her live, can he because she'd tell on him once he disappears with all that money and there's no way he's going to share it with her. Can't we help her?'

'We mustn't alter history, that's not why we're here, we're just onlookers not participants. We can't interfere with the past for our mission is to unlock the mystery of Polly's life so that we can give her back her name and help her soul rest in peace,' Charity replies as she masks her true pain, for she knows that Elsie's fate is to 'steal for love but die in despair', and this has to be, because her destiny is in the past and can't be altered by those from the future. 'We need to find Polly and discover how she fits into the equation along with the Uppinghams. Once we've done that we can return to the future, but remember, we're only onlookers, we mustn't interfere no matter what we see, for this is the past and has already been written in the book of history where it must remain.'

As they listen to Charity's words their hearts sink, for what she says is the truth but sometimes the truth doesn't always set you free and in this instance will lead to the death of an innocent, which they'll be powerless to prevent.

'Thank God Robyn managed to hire some 1940 clothes otherwise we'd stand out like a beacon amongst this lot,' says Monty jokingly, trying to bring some light into the darkness of the moment.

'We'll need to split up into three groups. Jack and I

89

will check out the Uppinghams. Sam and Lizzy, you need to get into the General's room and somehow take a copy of the list of securities in his safe as I've a feeling that list is going to be very important later on, leaving Robyn and you, my beloved, to find Polly.'

'Sounds good to me but we'll need to keep in contact and don't forget we must be back in time to open the portal again?' Suddenly Robyn pauses for a second. 'Oh my God, it's just dawned on me.'

'What? What's just dawned on you, my darling?' Aunt Lizzy cries as she begins to panic.

'The portal, we need an unbroken Ring of Power to open it up again and Leo's not here?' replies Robyn as they all stare at Charity.

She smiles that secret little grin of hers when she knows something they don't. 'Don't worry the RING will be complete.'

No more is said, for their love and trust in her is absolute as they agree to meet back in the ammunitions locker thirty minutes before the hour strikes midnight and the portal to the future is reopened.

'Look over there,' remarks Jack as he glances around, 'just behind that crate, it's a plan of the ship.'

They all rush towards it as they mentally make a note of the layout and mark out a safe place to meet, which is on the top deck behind the lifeboats should anyone find themselves in trouble before returning to the ammunition locker. Each of them notes the deck on which they think they'll find their charge and so begins the journey to find the truth aboard the HMS *Emperor*.

'Identify yourselves!'

Jack and Monty find themselves outside the Captain's quarters.

'This section's off limits to civilians. I repeat, identify yourselves immediately.'

They turn round to find a stocky stern-faced man aged about 40 wearing a naval uniform.

'We're with the Bank of England, you know, Mr Uppingham's staff, and we're looking for General Winkner's assistant Elsie, but got lost,' replies Monty hastily, thinking on his feet.

'Oh you mean Miss Pritchard, well you won't find her here, this is the Captain's deck and she's been billeted with the General's staff who are sharing quarters with the lower deck engineers. I thought you would know that being as you're sharing the same meals together?'

'Yeah but it's a bloody big ship and it's the first time we've had any free time to wander around it and lost our bearings,' replies Jack quickly before appealing to his ego. 'To be honest this is the first time we've ever been on a battleship and we were curious, I mean it's not everyday that blokes like us get to mix with the real heroes of the war who are actually in the thick of it. I don't suppose it would be possible for us to look around the ship with your permission of course.'

The officer smiles as he succumbs to Jack's charms. 'Security's very tight for obvious reasons but as you're with Mr Uppingham's team I suppose it'll be all right if I give you a basic tour of the old girl.'

'The old girl!' quips Monty.

'That's right, all ships are likened to women even when they're named after men like HMS *Emperor*. I'm First Officer Agar by the way and you are?'

'Monty and Jack, and as we said, we're with the Securities Manager Mr Uppingham, who's in charge of the transfer of the "you know what".' (Monty taps his nose indicating to Officer Agar that no more need be said). 'But we'd prefer it if you didn't let on that we'd been wandering around the ship as he can be a bit of a stickler.' Monty replies, hoping that he won't report them.

'I know what you mean, I've met him and he's worse than my Captain and that's saying something.'

They all laugh together while Officer Agar basks in the glory of being a 'war hero' as he introduces them to his fellow officers and shipmates while showing them around the ship. Monty and Jack follow him like little schoolboys relishing the excitement of actually being in a real battleship in the middle of the Atlantic during World War Two. It's a huge grey piece of steel with its weapons and guns of war all primed and ready to strike their deadly blows at Hitler's evil army as its men caress and watch over her like a lover who's eager to destroy any enemy that comes near her. They both look at each other and smile almost in disbelief at where they are, for if God had granted them one wish this would certainly be it; to experience a piece of history while it's actually happening. For a moment it crosses their minds that they've broken the rule of 'onlooker' by talking to the men on the ship but convince themselves that as long as they don't do anything to change the course of history then it's safe to continue indulging themselves for just a little longer. Finally the tour comes to an end as Officer Agar leaves them with the engineers in the lower deck.

'So you're with Führer Uppingham then,' jokes the engineers.

'I see you've got the measure of him,' Jack answers, seizing the opportunity to discover more about the family.

'You'd think that they were running this war the way they swan around as if they own the ship and everyone aboard. I mean no offence and all but he's just a glorified bank clerk and as for his so-called son, Harold, the snivelling little toad, if we had our way we'd put him in one of our guns and fire him back to Hitler.'

The laughter echoes around the billet as the engineers picture Harold flying through the air while Monty and Jack bask in the camaraderie of men bound together in war time.

'You don't have to tell us. He's worse than his father and the way he treats Elsie is despicable,' Monty says casually, hoping to glean more information.

'Little miss plain, I mean it's obvious he couldn't give a damn about her but she follows him around like a little mouse taking any little crumbs he throws at her. It's pathetic to watch but she's hooked on him bad and there's no getting away from that,' quips another engineer as a third pipes in:

'Don't forget the other one, what's her name, Polly? He's got her dangling on the side as well and she's far too pretty for prune-faced Harold. What is it about him that these women find so irresistible? It can't be his looks or charm. Here we are, a ship full of men, and the only women aboard, apart from Führer Uppingham's stone-faced wife Vera and Harold's twin sister, Hilary, who the devil himself wouldn't want, all fall for that snivelling little toad who doesn't even have the balls to fight in the war.'

'Who knows what women look for in men but you can bet money's at the root of it and they appear to have it,' replies Jack.

'You've hit it on the nail there. I heard him whispering to Polly the other day from their secret meeting place, the lifeboats, where they think we can't hear the noises coming from inside, that soon he'd be rich and then his parents wouldn't be able to stop him marrying her.'

'That's interesting, where's he going to get the money from? Certainly not Mr and Mrs Charm! They're not exactly the generous type if you get on the wrong side of them,' Monty remarks.

'Both Vera and Hilary hate Polly, that's for sure. I mean she's pretty and full of life and they're a couple of sour snobby cows who'll not allow a mere maid into the family circle so he's got to be plotting something with plain-faced Elsie because we can't see why he'd be hanging around her otherwise. He's that type, you've only got to look into those mean eyes of his and know that he's got some sort of plan up his sleeve. Though what she can do for him we're all still trying to fathom out. You wouldn't have any ideas on that score being as you work for them?'

All eyes are upon Monty and Jack as they wait for some juicy gossip.

'She's pretty tight with the Captain and he's in charge of the "cargo",' Jack replies while tapping his nose, indicating the other 'secret' cargo hidden amongst the weapons. 'So maybe she knows something that would benefit him.'

There's a long pause as the engineers glance at each other before one of them says,

'Nah, she's not bright enough to know anything and besides his father may be a second führer but there's no way he'd let anybody touch his precious cargo, not even his blue-eyed son Harold. I'm afraid you're barking up the wrong tree, mate, it's just a case of him being greedy. You know the type, can't settle for one woman but always has to have another on the side even if she is a bit plain. After all, he doesn't have the balls to fight Hitler like a real man so thinks being a ladies man makes him better than us. It really makes you want to land him in it.'

'What do you mean?' Monty asks, afraid that he already knows the answer.

'Someone should tell those poor girls what a rat he really is and then let's see how he talks his way out of that.'

They all laugh loudly as Monty and Jack look at each other realising that jealousy will be the catalyst that'll destroy all the lives entwined in this dark tale of betrayal, greed, lust and unrequited love. It's clear to them that one woman's betrayal will be another's destruction and ultimately they'll both pay a heavy price for the love of one man's evil heart. Soon one of these engineers will light the fuse that'll erupt into a volcano of fear and hate between these two women and they can do nothing to stop it for they are the outsiders in this tragic tale.

While Monty and Jack listen sorrowfully to the engineer's plan to discredit Harold, Sam and Aunt Lizzy are outside the General's room pondering how to gain access and steal a copy of the list of securities when the door opens...

'Who are you and what do you want?' Elsie asks nervously as her eyes betray her true feelings of guilt as she puts Harold's evil plan into action.

'Sorry, we didn't mean to startle you but we were looking for the General.'

'I'm his assistant, Miss Pritchard, and what is it that you require? The General isn't available at present.'

'We were hoping that he could help us with the inventory of the "other cargo", you know the one that's not officially logged,' replies Sam, winking at her. 'Just between us, we logged every entry of cargo for Mr Uppingham so that he could cross check against the General's list to make sure nothing was missing only we lost our list and if he finds out we'll lose our jobs. So we were hoping that the General would let us make a copy of his list, which we're sure would match Mr Uppingham's, and we could present that to him as our inventory.'

'It wouldn't be prudent to ask the General for a copy

of his list. If you did he would report you to Mr Uppingham immediately.'

'Oh please, isn't there something you can do? We're sure to lose our jobs and he wouldn't give us a reference, leaving our careers in ruins. Please, please say you'll help us as you're our last hope,' Sam implores, banking on the fact that she doesn't think much of Harold's father.

Elsie's brain ticks away quickly as she realises this could be a godsend in that if anything goes wrong with Harold's plan and the General and Mr Uppingham discover that the list of securities has been tampered with then the blame can be put on these two hapless employees.

'I wouldn't want you to lose your jobs and I know what a stinker Mr Uppingham can be. I'll help you as long as you promise never to tell anyone where you got the list from should anything go wrong and you get caught.'

'Agreed.'

She lets them in and proceeds to open the General's safe as the three of them surreptitiously copy the list of securities that'll destroy so many lives.

Meanwhile Charity and Robyn find themselves on deck by the lifeboats as they hear sounds coming from inside one of the boats.

'Oh, Harold, won't it be wonderful when we can finally be open about our relationship and are married with our own home.'

'My sweet Polly, how I love the way your nose twitches and your pretty little face comes alive when you're excited. You're like a precious china doll and how I adore you so.'

'Huh, I recognise that snake's voice,' whispers Robyn as they spot three naval engineers coming towards them while they quickly hide behind the lifeboats.

96

'How much longer must we go on like this, darling, as I'm sure your mother and sister already suspect something and they hate me, I know it? Can't we just tell your parents that we're in love and want to get married?'

The engineers stop by the lifeboats as they eavesdrop on the love-birds conversation, grinning devilishly between them.

'Hush, my little Petal, you must be patient. I've a plan that'll secure our future together and then it won't matter what my parents think or do.'

'What plan, Harold?'

'No need for you to worry your pretty little head about anything, my darling, you just have to be patient, and as for my sister and mother, they won't do anything to hurt me. You just leave everything to me and dream about our future life together.'

While the force and sound of their lovemaking erupts through the lifeboats the engineers stand by sniggering as Charity and Robyn look on.

'That poor girl, if only she knew what a rat he really is,' whispers Robyn, her body cringing at the thought of Harold's slimy hands all over her.

Charity looks at the engineers and sees into their souls and knows that they're about to light the fuse that'll ignite the powerful force of jealousy within Polly's heart. Soon the beast will awaken from within her and the dark side of Polly will erupt.

'What is it, Charity?' Robyn asks, feeling her pain.

'Whatever happens now we can't interfere! Remember, we're only here to discover the truth.'

'What's going to happen?' she cries...

Suddenly the engineers move closer to the lifeboats and so begins the journey into betrayal and despair.

'Did you see that Harold making love to the General's assistant the other night. I mean, you'd think he'd be a bit more careful, especially as he's also romancing the maid,' says the first engineer loudly, ensuring that the love-birds overhear him as the second one continues:

'Yeah and he spits out the same rubbish to both of them and they believe him, the poor cows.'

The third continues their tawdry tale: 'Especially the maid, what's her name, Polly, I mean the poor girl thinks that he's going to marry her, but when you hear him extolling his undying love to the General's assistant, Elsie, it's her he's going to marry.'

The first engineer completes the trap that'll ensure Harold's demise. 'Well I heard him bragging to one of the officers the other night that he's got the maid wrapped around his little finger and that she'll do anything for him but it's Elsie who's going to secure his future.'

'What a slime ball,' says the second engineer as they make their way back to their quarters, smirking contentedly to themselves as they wait for Harold's nightmare to begin.

The silence in the air is deafening as Charity and Robyn watch Harold and Polly slowly emerge from their love-nest until they're standing beside each other. Polly's beautiful face now tortured with the pain of betrayal. Her eyes filled with hatred as the tears flow and she glares at him, while her magnificent mane of long silky brown hair flows wildly in the wind that's suddenly erupted from within the calmness of a sunny June day. Harold can barely look at her as he desperately tries to think of a way to redeem himself. Their bodies stand coldly apart without a word passing between them as monstrous black clouds eclipse the sun above and the skies open up into thunderous rainfall that drenches their bodies as the wind continues to howl bitterly all around them.

'Don't look at me like that Polly, I can't bare it.'

'You can't bare it! You betray my love and then stand there and say you can't bare it! How could I've been so blind and stupid as not to see you for what you really are, your father's son? I see now that a mere maid could never be accepted as an equal into the Uppingham dynasty and that your future is with the plain yet far more well connected General's assistant. Why not have your way with me while waiting for your other bride to secure your future. What was she going to do for you, Harold? What has she got that you need so badly that you'd betray my love?'

The words pour out from Polly's mouth with such venom that even Harold, with his cold calculating heart, cowers in the wind and rain as he tries to defend his betrayal.

'It's not like they say, you must believe me. I never said those words to the officer, they're lying. They're jealous of me. It's you I love, not Elsie. I'm using her to secure our future. You must trust me, Polly, I love you and only you, but I can't live without money and my father will disinherit me when we marry. Remember I told you I had a plan that would make us rich. Well Elsie's the key and once I have got what I need from her then we can be together for ever my beautiful Polly. Trust me, I love you, only you.'

'You got to hand it to him, even when he's been caught red-handed he still proclaims his love for her,' whispers Robyn as Charity says:

'I believe that he truly does love her, but his greed will be his destruction.'

'Why, what do you see?'

'Darkness I'm afraid, my dear Robyn, darkness.'

'What a liar you are. You lie to me and to her and what for? Money and power. That's all you Uppinghams live for nothing else matters to you. Well let's see how your precious Elsie will feel about helping you when I tell her about us.'

'No, no, you mustn't Polly, please don't do anything hasty, you'll ruin everything. I need her for the list, once I've got the list then we can be together,' he begs, trying to draw closer as the wind cuts through him with such a force that he can barely move. The deck is awash with rain while they struggle against the elements.

'What list?' she yells.

'The list of securities that the General has in his safe. Once I have the list I can alter it and we will have two million pounds. Just think, Polly, two million pounds. We'll be rich. But I need Elsie to get me the list. Trust me, Polly, it's you I love, not her. I just need the list then we'll be together I promise.'

Polly stops for a moment and looks into his eyes and for a second she sees he's telling the truth, but his betrayal cuts too deep and her love has turned to bitter hatred, which has awoken the beast within.

'I'll destroy them both,' she thinks to herself as she feels the power of the beast flow within her.

'I need to see proof of your love.'

'Anything, my love, you've only to ask and it shall be done,' he replies, little realising that those words will be his undoing as he begins to feel safe once more.

'Bring me the list once you have altered it, Harold, and show me what you've done. Only then will I believe you truly love me.'

For a second he hesitates as his plan was for him alone to know the identity of the false accounts so that only he can claim the £2 million. But his arrogance once again gets the better of him as he believes that once more Polly has succumbed to his irresistible charm. So he agrees. The rain suddenly stops and the wind disappears into the air as the sun flickers through the dispersing clouds while he holds her in his arms whispering his undying love. She smiles secretly to herself, waiting for the moment when revenge will be hers.

8

The Dark Side

Sam and Lizzy finish copying the list, while Elsie makes sure the coast is clear.

'Thank you, Elsie, you've saved our bacon and if ever you need our help,' says Sam, not realising that one day, not too far in the future, those words will come back to haunt her.

'No problem, but remember, I didn't give you the list if you get caught,' she replies as she closes the door and returns to complete her copy for Harold, whom she's agreed to meet later that evening by the lifeboats, Harold's favourite meeting place for his rendezvous.

'Where have you been, son? You're late. You know that we're having dinner with the Captain and General tonight and how important it is that we present the right impression,' bellows Harold's father as Vera fusses around making sure his suit fits correctly, while Hilary can't wait to find out what her beloved twin brother's been up to. Although they're not identical, their heart and soul are as one and whatever Harold is plotting Hilary is sure to be deep in there with him.

'Don't worry, father, I won't let the side down, besides the General will be so drunk that he won't remember what day it is let alone whether anyone has arrived late.'

'Watch your tongue, my boy, and have respect for your elders,' retorts his father as Hilary sniggers away, and they all try to get dressed in the cramped cabin quarters that they're forced to share, which is far beneath their normal standards.

'Where's Polly?' yells Vera as she attempts to fix her hair. 'That girl is useless and as soon as we arrive in Canada I'm going to have her replaced.'

'But she'll be stranded in a strange country without any friends or money,' retorts Harold sharply.

'Well she'd better perk her ideas up then.'

'Sometimes, mother, I don't think you have a heart, just a cold vessel that blood runs through,' replies Harold, for in his own way he does love Polly, but he loves money and power more, which is why he'll betray her and Elsie when he's done with them. There's only one person he truly cares for, Hilary, who shares all his dark secrets and who, like he, will betray all that is sacred in her thirst for power and riches.

'Where have you been, girl? I need you to press my dress for this evening.'

'Sorry, Mrs Uppingham, I was collecting all the washing from the laundry room as you said you needed it urgently,' replies Polly apologetically as she rushes in carrying bags of heavy laundry, which no one offers to help her with. Hilary and Harold grin at each other as their parents bully her mercilessly.

'Sixty pounds a year isn't enough for the way these people treat me, but soon I'll have my revenge on them all,' she thinks, as she smiles secretly to herself. She looks over at Harold to see him whispering clandestinely with Hilary in the corner, suddenly seeing them for what they really are, cold and amoral. 'That's right, Harold, plot away with your sister, for soon the both of you will know what betrayal really is,' she contemplates, humming to herself as she presses Mrs Uppingham's dress, waiting for her time to come.

'You sound happy, Polly, must be love?' smirks Hilary.

'I wouldn't know about love, Miss Uppingham, that seems to be reserved for my betters.'

'At last, a sensible comment, there may be hope for you yet, girl,' says Mrs Uppingham cruelly as Polly helps her with her dress. 'Don't forget to tidy up the cabin and sort out the laundry, oh, and we may need you when we get back so don't go to bed.'

'What time will that be, Mrs Uppingham?'

'I don't know, girl, it's not your place to ask questions, just do what you're told.'

Harold winks at her as they prepare to leave, mouthing silently that he'll meet her at their secret place after dinner tonight.

'Good evening, Captain, General, and may I thank you on behalf of my family for your kind invitation.'

'Not at all, Mr Uppingham, I thought it would be appropriate for you to meet all the other officers and for them to meet you and your family so that everyone is aware of their positions aboard ship.'

'Excellent idea, Captain, as it's a rather large vessel and considering the "special cargo" we're carrying it is indeed pertinent that we all know who's who otherwise mistakes can be made.'

'Indeed, Mr Uppingham, security is paramount,' comments the General, who's already unsteady on his feet. Elsie stands at his side, protecting him as usual, smiling coyly at Harold. Hilary nudges his shoulder, relishing the thought of both her rivals having their hearts broken. Her love for her twin brother goes deeper and darker than that of a sister as she covets him above

104

all others and sees all other women, even her own mother, as a threat. To Hilary there is only one true love in her life, Harold, and any woman that takes him away from her is her enemy. But for now she consoles herself with the knowledge that these two pathetic creatures are but pawns in their evil plan for the future and that his love for her transcends all others.

'Did you get the list, my Petal?' whispers Harold to Elsie as they make their way to the dinner table.

'Yes, my love, it's in my room.'

He breathes a sigh of relief as he squeezes her hand under the table. 'We'll meet up in your room after dinner and celebrate our future together.'

The evening wears on as they all brag how Hitler will soon surrender once all the monies are deposited in Canada, and Britain can buy enough weapons from America to defeat him.

"You've got to hand it to Churchill, his plan to empty the nation's wealth and ship it to a safe haven in Canada is brilliant, if not mad, but if it should fail, well the consequences are too....'

'Failure is not a word that Churchill or anyone on this ship would even contemplate, General,' snaps Roland Uppingham in that superior British tone of his, which makes the General isolated and alone as all eyes are suddenly upon him.

'Of course not, I was just...'

'Have another drink, General, and then everything will look much better,' jokes Harold in that cold manner of his, which brings Elsie up sharp as she looks straight into his eyes and for the first time doesn't like what she sees.

'You've got a heavy schedule planned for tomorrow, General, so perhaps an early night would be beneficial,' she says protectively.

He looks around the room and sees that she's right,

it's time to make an exit before the demon drink takes him over completely.

'A general is never off duty I'm afraid, but my assistant is right, an early night is called for, so I bid you goodnight ladies and gentlemen.'

As Elsie and the General make their exit, Harold winks at her, while Hilary looks on icily before he makes his excuses and wings his way along to her cabin to collect his prize; the list.

Back at the lifeboats the RING meet up and exchange stories.

'What do we do now?' Robyn asks as they check their watches and realise that they've only two more hours until midnight when the portal must be opened again.

'We wait and watch, for this is where Polly's journey into oblivion begins,' replies Charity.

'What do you see, Spud?' asks Monty who can sense the pain and anguish in her voice.

'Within the hour we'll see what darkness befalls those who seek life's happiness through the eyes of the beast when betrayal, greed and lust become their master.'

'I don't think I want to know the answer.'

'I know, Sam, but sometimes in seeking the truth, pain is your companion.'

'Sometimes being your friend can be hard.' Charity smiles as they hide within the shadows of this great battleship, waiting for destiny.

Harold taps on Elsie's cabin door as he looks around unaware that Hilary has followed him, for her jealousy has grown so dark that she can no longer control her own emotions. She knows that her beloved twin wouldn't betray her, but still she can't help herself and watches from the shadows as he's greeted by a passionate kiss from his lover. The demon beast within her tortured soul awakes and feeds on her jealousy and lust as the door closes and her imagination takes over.

'Oh Harold, I'm so afraid, what if we get caught?'

'Nothing will go wrong, my Petal, you're safe now.'

He kisses her with such force that she collapses in his embrace, her heart beating so fast that she can barely breathe. His hands run all over her body, while he closes his eyes and pictures the future full of the riches that'll soon be his and his alone. Hilary watches from the cabin porthole as her dark side gains control.

'The list, my Petal, where is it?' he whispers as he continues to make passionate love, but in his heart it's not her body that he's caressing, but Polly's, as his passions are aroused to such heights that they become as one. She cries out with such ecstasy that Hilary becomes so enraged that she draws blood from her lip as she tries to contain the beast within.

'I've never experienced such love before, Harold.'

He smiles that secret grin of his. If only she knew whose body he was really caressing. They get dressed and then Elsie presents him with his prize: the list. He looks through it, slowly soaking up its power, and then holds it close to his chest as he closes his eyes and dreams of his future. At last he'll be free of his oppressive father and domineering mother. At last he'll be free to be whatever he wants. For a moment it crosses his mind that Polly could fit into his new life, but his dark side takes over as greed enters his soul. Hilary watches as she sees his face light up, and Elsie sitting beside him talking incessantly of their future together and how wonderful it will be. The blood flows from her lips as she bites deeper into them and her invidious resentment of her rival possesses her completely until she erupts into a blinding rage. She bangs on the cabin door, screaming. Elsie opens it and she rushes in, her body shaking uncontrollably.

'He'll never marry you or Polly, you're just a means to an end, and now he has the list you're excess baggage.'

Elsie's mind explodes into a minefield of emotions as she struggles to comprehend Hilary's bitter words.

'I don't understand, what does Polly have to do with us? What's going on, Harold?' She looks at him in bewilderment, her body shaking with fear, while Hilary collapses into hysterical laughter as she realises what she's done.

'Nothing's going on, my love.'

'Then why's Hilary so upset, tell me, Harold?'

'You've served your purpose and your services are no longer required. That's what's going on, little miss boring,' scowls Hilary as Harold strikes her across the face in a fit of blind rage. He sees his future being destroyed by her jealousy. She shrivels back into the corner of the cabin holding her face as she looks up at him and sees the hate in his eyes and her heart breaks as the tears flow. She's lost his love and destroyed their future together. What'll become of her now that her beloved twin has turned against her?

'What purpose?' Elsie cries as she sees her lover's true soul clearly for the first time. Cold, dark and calculating.

'Don't listen to her ramblings, my love, she's full of jealousy. She can't bare the thought that I love you so much and that my future is with you.'

'Stop it. I see you now and oh what a fool I've been. "Served my purpose", what fun the two of you must've had laughing at me, while I foolishly believed your lies of undying love? So, Harold, now that you have the list what about Polly, where does she fit into your plans?

What can she do for you? Surely a maid has nothing to offer but her body.'

He turns his head away, unable to look her straight in the eyes, and her heart breaks as she realises.

'You love her. You make love to me but it's her you desire. Well you can have her, but she gets you, as you are, disgraced and poor. The list that you worked so hard to obtain will be worthless once I tell the General of your plan.'

'If you tell him then you lose as you're the one that stole it, not me, and it's your reputation that'll be ruined, not mine, as I made sure that there's no link to me. No one knows about us and I'll deny everything,' he replies coldly as his dark side takes hold and is already telling him that there's only one way out of this nightmare if his plan is to be saved.

'You think I care about what happens to me now? How little you really understand women. My future has already been destroyed. All I have left now is the one thing you covet the most, your precious list. I may lose everything, but you'll not have your riches and see if your precious Polly will marry you then.'

'Stop her, Harold, stop her now,' shouts Hilary as she tries to redeem herself.

'Shut up, you bitch. Haven't you done enough?' he yells as her body crumples under his cruel words and she suddenly sees the blackness of her life before her. By destroying Elsie and Polly she's destroyed herself and her beloved brother. There's no greater betrayal than that of a sister's blind love for her brother.

'I beg you don't do this, for you'll leave me no choice,' he pleads, as he looks into her eyes and sees the emptiness that's replaced the passion that once looked back at him.

She stands still, her eyes dead, as she awaits her fate.

'It's too late, Harold, there's no where for me to go. I choose truth. What do you choose?'

His body goes cold as he knows what he must do. She stands still and lifeless waiting for him to choose, her heart broken by his betrayal. He moves towards her and their bodies touch as he places his hands around her shoulders, pulling her close to him while whispering in her ear, 'You leave me no choice, my Petal. What am I to do? I have no choice.' His hands slowly make their way to her neck as she stands completely motionless, her eyes showing the pain of betrayal as he coldly chokes the life from her. No words pass between them as her body slumps to the ground and she looks up at him accusingly. Her eyes close and the last breath of life finally leaves her body as the demon of death passes into his soul and marks his future for all eternity.

'What have you done?' Hilary cries.

'You mean we, don't you,' he retorts as the spirit of death shows him a glimpse of his future. A dark demonic place where he can hear his own cries of pain, but there's no one to help him. He's alone, without friendship or love, where evil demons and spirits torment him with their dark satanic cries of despair. Something touches his shoulder as he turns around quickly, but there's nothing there, except a voice, an evil demonic voice whispering, 'Welcome to the dark side, Harold, I've been waiting for you.'

'Did you hear that?' he shouts as he moves around the cabin, his eyes darting everywhere as his body trembles uncontrollably.

'Hear what?' she replies, looking around her as his fear becomes hers and she senses that something terrible is about to happen.

'I didn't plan to kill her, you made me do it. It's your fault. You're the murderer, not me. Why did you do it?

110

Everything was going so well. See what you've done, you bitch. You've ruined everything. Now what do we do?' His voice rambles in a state of panic as he tries to rationalise his murderous actions, but he can't escape this evil presence all around him, and the voice keeps whispering, 'Welcome to the dark side, Harold, I've been waiting for you.'

'I'm sorry, I'm sorry, Harold, please say you forgive me. I can't bear it if you turn against me. We can fix it. It'll be all right. Just give me a few minutes to think.'

'It's a pity you didn't think earlier, then we wouldn't be in this mess,' he yells, still hearing voices as Hilary's beast returns with a vengeance and her dark side takes over as she thinks of a way out and the opportunity to redeem herself with Harold.

'This was meant to be. Elsie would never have let you go with the money. She would have betrayed you as will Polly. There can be no witnesses, Harold.'

He pauses for a moment as his soul sinks further into the dark side.

'You're right, I can't trust anyone. There's too much at stake. But how do we get rid of the body and what do I do with Polly? If she doesn't see the list later tonight with the adjustments she'll betray me like Elsie was going to.'

'No one knows about you and Elsie, although I have my suspicions that mother knows about you and Polly, but we can deal with her later. First we need to get rid of the body.' Then instantly it comes to her. 'We'll throw it overboard. We're in the middle of the Atlantic ocean, there couldn't be a more perfect place for a body or two to disappear.'

'Of course, Sis,' he mutters. 'The perfect murder.'

'Exactly, Harold, no bodies, no crime and an entire ocean to lose them in.'

111

They look at each, smiling coldly, as the beast within them takes over and they sink deeper and deeper into the dark side.

'Bodies, Sis,' he replies, hesitating for a moment, but already his dark heart is one step ahead of her.

'There can be no witnesses, Harold.'

'Poor Polly, such a pretty little thing, and I do love her in my own way, but needs must, Sis, needs must,' he replies as the two of them instigate the next stage of their amended plan.

Quickly they wrap the body in a bed sheet and clean the cabin of any traces of their presence before carefully checking that the decks are clear and dragging her lifeless body to the edge of the ship. As Hilary keeps lookout, Harold struggles to lift her ample frame.

'Did I really make love to this lump of lard?' he mutters callously under his breath as he finally manages to throw her lifeless body overboard, being careful to keep the sheet. The waters splash with the thunderous sound of her body sinking into the abyss as the two of them watch, without compassion or remorse, while the fish tear furiously at this unexpected feast. Soon they're far away as the ship moves swiftly through the waters and the most heinous crime of all is hidden in the depths of the sea.

'Poor little Elsie, such an innocent in life's cruel game,' laments Harold as the two of them return to her cabin. Hilary remakes the bed with the same sheet as Harold goes through the list and replaces two sheets with the same page numbers, 12 and 13, which he carefully forged at the Bank of England from his father's list. This is identical to the General's except for the six bogus accounts that appear randomly on the sheets each containing a sixth of £2 million (three on each sheet). Harold destroys the original pages 12 and 13, and then shows Hilary his other list, which contains the six account numbers plus the labyrinth of bogus accounts that he's already set up in Switzerland before leaving England, and into which the £2 million will automatically be transferred over the next six months, once the list is delivered to the secret location in Montreal. The beauty of his plan is that he doesn't have to do anything. The list and other bank staff will do the work for him. All he has to do is sit back and wait. Then, when the final monies have been transferred both he and Hilary can disappear before the auditors arrive to do the financial year end in March. They both grin smugly as they dream of collecting the £2 million and beginning their new life.

'Now all I need to do is show my list to Polly and then we're home free,' he says, smiling as he tucks it into his coat pocket before they close the cabin door behind them. While making their way back to their cabin, Hilary coldly points out:

'Do you need to show Polly the list, wouldn't it be better just to kill her straight away?'

'Don't worry, I know what I'm doing. I'll deal with Polly. Murder is easier second time around,' he says icily, as a dark shadowy figure, half man, half beast, crosses their path, smiling devilishly, mesmerising them with his blood-red eyes and fixating them with his evil stare. Their bodies freeze with terror. They've crossed over into the dark side, which holds a future that's not paved with riches but cloaked in death and despair. Their own!

9

Ice-Olation

'Did you see it?'

'What was it, Harold? What does it want with us?' Hilary replies, her body alive with fear as her mind races with dark thoughts that she tries to erase. But they won't leave her alone as she cradles her head in her hands with her eyes shut tight as darker and darker images flash before her of an evil place full of tormented souls that keep calling to her. 'Come, Hilary, join us. The Master is waiting.'

'Stop them, Harold, stop them, I'm afraid. What have we done?' she cries as they both hold each other tightly.

'It's too late, Sis,' he replies as he can no longer deny their fate. 'We've blood on our souls and the clock of time is ticking and soon he'll collect.'

'Who'll collect? I didn't murder anyone. There's no blood on my soul. I'm not guilty,' she cries as he looks at her coldly.

'We're as one in body and soul, my dear twin, and what I feel you feel. My hands may have choked the life from Elsie, but your thoughts put them there. Our fates are bound together and there's no escape.'

It's 10 p.m. and they're standing by the lifeboats as the RING hide in the shadows, watching and waiting.

'Polly mustn't see you. Go back to the cabin, I won't be long.'

'I'm not leaving,' retorts Hilary sharply. 'I don't trust her, she's tougher than Elsie and besides you care for her. It won't be so easy to kill her as you did Elsie.'

'Did you hear that they've murdered Elsie?' whispers Sam as Aunt Lizzy holds her hand, trying to hold back the tears as the others look on silently.

'They're evil, she wasn't bad, just innocent and lonely.'

'I know, Sam,' says Charity, 'but her destiny was already decided and there's nothing we could've done to change that.'

'It doesn't make it right though, does it?'

'I know, I know,' Charity replies, feeling completely powerless.

'A minute ago you were pleading that your soul is free of Elsie's blood and now you can't wait to destroy Polly. Sometimes I don't understand you, Sis. One minute you're crying for forgiveness and the next you're craving the blood of another.'

'I can't help it, I love you so much, Harold, that anyone or anything that threatens our future together is our enemy and must be destroyed.'

'But Polly isn't my enemy, she loves me, and we could be happy together. Don't you want me to be happy, Sis?'

'She's not right for you. She doesn't understand you like I do. She doesn't see your true soul. It's dark, Harold, like mine. We were born of the same seed split into two. We were meant to be together forever. No one will love or understand you better than I...'

'How touching. A sister's love it appears knows no boundaries.'

'Polly, I didn't hear you coming, how long have you been here?' Harold asks sheepishly.

'Long enough to know that Hilary's love will destroy you. It's a selfish love that sees only her way or no way.'

'You bitch, you're nothing, you're not worthy of him. You never were. He's destined for better things...'

'With you by his side no doubt?'

'Stop it, stop it, I can't abide this bickering. Sis, leave us alone, I need to talk to Polly.'

'But Harold.'

'No buts, leave us,' he shouts.

Hilary slumps off, but only goes round the corner out of view, as she watches Polly move closer to Harold until their bodies are entwined and they kiss passionately. She can feel the demon beast raging within her, only this time her hatred of Polly is such that she can barely contain herself. Harold's body weakens as he succumbs to Polly's passion, while she thinks only of revenge.

'Oh Polly, I do love you. I really do.'

Hilary's eyes flash with hatred as Polly asks, 'The list, Harold, did you get the list?'

Harold laughs as he senses that she's more like him than Hilary realises.

'Yes, my Petal.'

He puts his hand in his pocket and shows her his 'future', for soon he knows what he must do as her kisses betray her true feelings. His heart is heavy, for although he knows her words are false, he can still feel her love as he kisses her one last time before 'death is her prize'. Their lips touch with such a force that blood is drawn and Hilary can bear it no longer, as once again, the demon beast erupts and she charges towards them.

'You can't have him. He's mine,' she yells as she leaps out from the shadows. They both turn in horror to see this demon woman raging uncontrollably towards them.

'Stop, Sis, stop.' But it's too late as her body crashes against theirs and they both tumble over the edge of the ship, clinging onto the side.

'My God, she's mad. She's trying to kill them both,'

screams Robyn as Charity holds her back, while the rest of the RING struggle to contain their feelings.

'We must help them, Spud. We can't just let them die.'

'No, honey, we mustn't interfere. This isn't our time. We're from the future. Their destiny has already been foretold.'

'But it's murder. We can't stand by,' yells Robyn as she pulls away from Charity and rushes out towards them.'

'Stop her, honey, we mustn't alter the course of history,' Charity begs Monty as they all dash after Robyn. Polly and Harold are hanging on by a thread as Hilary tries to pull Harold up, while Robyn dashes towards Polly.

'Grab my hand,' she cries as Jack and Monty follow in quick pursuit until all three are trying to save her. Sam and Aunt Lizzy struggle with their conscience as they stand by with Charity, who's shouting:

'Please stop, please stop, we mustn't interfere.'

But it's too late as Jack and Monty pull Polly up, while Hilary screams, 'No, not her, save Harold, save him.'

His hand starts to slip from hers as Jack and Monty rush to grab him, but they're too late. Hilary's strength gives out and she watches him fall into the cruel seas as he looks up at her, his eyes full of hate and terror. Hate for what she's done and terror at the fate that awaits him in the 'Dark Life'.

'Thank you. You've saved my life, how can I ever repay you?'

Robyn, Jack and Monty stand silently, afraid to speak. They feel Charity's eyes upon them as the sudden realisation of what they've done begins to dawn on them.

'He's dead, he's dead. You bitch, it's your fault. Why didn't you save him? Why? Why? Why?' yells Hilary hysterically, the tears flowing uncontrollably down her cheeks as she looks at the RING accusingly, while they slowly gather around until the two women are standing in the centre. Polly sees something white fall from her pocket and bends down to pick it up as Hilary spots it.

'Give that to me, you cow, it's Harold's,' she screams as she tries to grab it from Polly's hand.

'Let go, let go, you murderess,' shouts Polly as Hilary is stunned by her words.

'It was an accident. I didn't mean for him to die. It should have been you. It's not my fault. You took him with you. You're the murderess, not me. I tried to save him. I loved him. I loved him. Give me the list, it's mine.'

They tear at each other, pulling their hair and scratching as they scream and yell abuse, while the RING look on in horror until finally Polly wins and Hilary is left bruised and beaten on the floor. Polly puts the list back in her pocket as Hilary slowly pulls herself together until she's standing upright, facing her enemy. She wipes the tears and blood from her battered and scratched face before swearing vengeance.

'I'll destroy you, Polly Melrose, you'll pay, a life for a life.' She turns until her eyes are fixed upon the RING. 'You'll all pay.' Then with a deep breath she screams, 'Help, help, she's murdered him. Please help me.' The ship comes alive with the sound of running feet as Hilary continues her screams of despair.

'We can't be found here, we must go now,' shouts Charity.

'Please don't leave me. Help me, please?' Polly begs as Hilary's screams get louder and the crew are nearly upon them.

'Come with us,' Sam says quickly, while grabbing Polly's arm as they all run back to the ammunition locker. Jack locks the door behind them as they listen to the frantic sound of the crew searching.

Monty checks his watch, catching his breath. 'We've got another twenty-five minutes before it's midnight and we can open the portal.'

'It'll be a miracle if they don't find us before then.'

'Your usual positive self, Jack?' quips Robyn.

'Haven't you done enough without all this squabbling?'

'Sorry, Charity, we didn't mean anything by it,' replies Robyn as they all look sheepish, knowing that they have done wrong and she's angry with them.

'Who are you and where have you come from?' Polly interrupts as she tries to make sense of it all. For once everyone is speechless as they all look to Charity.

'It's a long story, but let's just say that we're not from this time, but we know who you are and have come to help you.'

'Help me, how? I don't know you yet somehow I feel I do. It's really weird, I know we've never met yet I feel we have. Am I going mad and is this all a dream? Please tell me it's a dream and that I'll soon wake up to find Harold alive and we're still in love and none of this nightmare with Elsie and Hilary happened.'

No one answers as they all look down, fearful of telling her the whole truth. 'This isn't a dream is it and Harold is really dead and I'm going to be accused of his murder aren't I?'

Charity can barely hold back the tears as she tries to comfort her. 'No it's not a dream and Harold is dead and I'm afraid you'll pay a heavy price for loving him, but the truth will set you free. Trust us when I say we've come to help you, but not in the way you think. You'll have to believe in us as we do in you.'

Polly looks into Charity's eyes and the connection is made. 'I believe you although I don't understand or know why, but somehow I feel you're my friend and my saviour. What shall I do, for there's no way off this ship, and

119

your friend is right, it won't be long before they get round to searching this place?'

Charity and the RING are silent as their brains race against time to not only save Polly, but also themselves.

'They've killed them and thrown their bodies overboard,' cries Hilary hysterically, as her parents try to calm her down, while the Captain and General look on.

'Killed who, my darling?' her mother asks as she holds her in her arms.

'Harold and Elsie, mother. Polly and the others killed them both.'

'No, that can't be right. You're mistaken. Harold can't be dead?' her mother screams as her father takes over.

'What do you mean, Polly, and the others? Who are these others and why would they want to kill Harold and Elsie?'

'The list, father, they wanted the list.'

'What list?'

'The list of securities. Elsie and Harold were secret lovers and the two of them were checking that the bank's and the General's lists matched. They used to meet in her cabin and tonight, after dinner, met up as usual only this time they decided to double check the lists, just in case there were any errors. They were both very conscientious, father, and wanted to make sure that everything was in order before the ship docked in Canada.'

'Elsie would have told me if she and Harold were lovers. She didn't keep secrets from me,' retorts the General, his body shaking with shock as he runs his tongue along his lips desperate for a drink. Elsie looked after and protected him. What will he do now that she's dead? He'll be lost without her. He loved her like a daughter and can't believe that she won't be sitting at her tiny desk in the morning making him black coffee and arranging his day. If Polly murdered her then, by God, he'll leave no stone unturned until she's been brought to book along with her conspirators.

'I still don't understand how Polly's involved?' the Captain asks as he studies Hilary's body language and isn't convinced, like the others, that she's entirely innocent.

'She was jealous of Elsie. She was in love with Harold and kept pestering him, but he was only interested in Elsie and told her so. She became increasingly erratic and followed Harold to Elsie's cabin.'

The Captain was becoming suspicious of her story, which didn't quite add up.

'How do you know all this?'

'Harold told me about their affair and Polly during dinner tonight. We agreed to meet up in Elsie's cabin to talk about how they were going to deal with her increasing jealousy. When I arrived I found Polly banging on the cabin door screaming. When Elsie opened the door she started hitting her and calling her names. Elsie got frightened and ran off in tears with Polly chasing after her. Harold and I followed them until Elsie stopped by the lifeboats. The next thing, Polly leapt at her in a fit of rage and pushed her over the side, but she managed to cling onto the side of the ship, screaming for help. Harold rushed to grab Elsie's hand and that's when Polly hit him over the head with a steel bar, which was on the deck by the lifeboat. He fell to the ground when suddenly these people arrived from nowhere, yet they seemed to know Polly as she screamed at them, "Help me. I've got the other list. If you help me kill them then you can have it." Within seconds they were helping Polly murder Elsie and Harold. Polly then picked up the steel bar and threw it out to sea.'

'That's convenient, so we don't have the murder weapon

121

and the only witness to the crime is you, Miss Uppingham. Why didn't you help your brother and Elsie?' the Captain interrupts, not convinced with Hilary's description of events.

'Who are these "mysterious people" that Polly seems to know and what's this other list?'

'How dare you question my daughter in that tone? Her brother, my son, has just been brutally murdered by our maid and her accomplices and you more or less accuse her. You should be out there looking for my son's killers,' yells her mother as Hilary smiles secretly to herself, knowing that the Captain's no match for either of her parents.

'That's right, Captain, my daughter isn't the guilty one here and we're wasting time,' shouts her father as the General agrees with him, while still desperately wanting a drink to get him through this nightmare now that he hasn't got his Elsie to look out for him.

'I'm just trying to get the full picture here, Mr Uppingham. Two things puzzle me. What's this "other list" and who are these people that no one seems to know about? I run a tight ship and I'd know if there were unauthorised persons aboard.'

'Well, if they're unauthorised you wouldn't know about them now would you, Captain, which means you let murderers aboard your ship and I'll see you court-martialled for this when we arrive in Canada.'

'You're understandably upset, Mr Uppingham,' replies the Captain, suddenly feeling very vulnerable and afraid for his position. 'Of course, you're right, our main priority is to find the killers. Once we've done that then we can establish the motives, because there seems to be more than one, Polly's jealousy and this "other list" that her accomplices were after.'

Hilary sits, worried by the Captain's last words, for

when they do find Polly she'll be able to tell them about Harold's plan. She can't afford for that to happen so somehow must get to her before they do.

Her father, the Captain and General leave to join the search as Hilary frantically tries to think where Polly might hide, while her mother crumples into a crying heap.

'Here you are, mother, take this, it'll help you.' Hilary gives her a drink of whisky laced with a sleeping pill that will knock her out for hours. As her mother sleeps, she paces the cabin, trying to think. 'Of course, the ammunition locker, Harold's other meeting place for his lovers.' Quickly she searches her father's desk for his pistol, which he keeps for protection, and then races to destroy her enemy.

'Polly, you'll have to take Leo's place in the Ring of Power,' Charity says excitedly as she sees now that Polly's past is intrinsically linked to their present.

'Nice one, Spud,' shouts Monty as he checks his watch again to see that the midnight hour is but a few minutes away.

'I don't understand, what do you mean take Leo's place?' Polly asks, suddenly feeling very afraid.

'Now I know this is going to sound incredible, but you've just got to trust us. We come from the future and have been sent back to help you. You live for another sixty-five years and die aged eighty-five, but your soul is in the balance and I've been charged with an effort to save it. We've met in the future, Polly. That's why you already feel you know me. You will survive tonight, but unless we can return to our time there will be no future for any of us. Will you help us?'

No one moves or speaks as Polly struggles to comprehend what's happening, but as she looks into the panic-stricken faces of these strangers she feels strangely comforted and instantly knows what she must do.

'I don't understand what's happening to me but somehow feel compelled to help you.'

'We must hurry, Jack, grab that box and place it in the centre so I can lay out the cards of Thor while the rest of you form the Ring of Power. Polly, soon you'll see a portal open within the room. Don't be afraid, it's a gateway back to our time. But the cards must not be broken until I enter last. When the hand of time strikes eight minutes past midnight then you must gather the cards in this order placing them in this box and then throw the box to me.'

'What about me? You can't leave me here?'

'The angels of Thor will protect you. Remember what I told you. You'll survive tonight. Trust me, Polly. Trust me.'

As the hour strikes midnight and Charity begins to recite the ancient tongue of Thor the room transforms into a huge open void as his golden angels enter through the portal. Polly is transfixed as one by one the angels carry the RING into the portal and back through time until only Charity remains. Suddenly the door breaks down and the Captain, his men, the General and Uppingham rush in to find themselves frozen in disbelief at what they see. A huge golden angel floating before them holding Charity protectively in its left hand as it wields its mighty golden sword in the other with its magnificent wings spread high above as it looks down upon everyone.

'The cards, Polly, gather the cards as I showed you, hurry, there isn't much time. Hurry, Polly, hurry,' Charity shouts, waking Polly from her trance.

'What the fuck's going on?' shouts one of the officers as Hilary sneaks in behind him until she's got Polly within her sight.

124

'Watch your mouth,' yells the Captain while making the sign of the cross as the General and Uppingham stare open mouthed at the apparition before them.

'What evil is this?' Upppingham shouts as he sees Polly about to open the box. 'That's her, that's my son's killer, don't let her get away.'

Hilary seizes her chance and points the pistol straight at Polly and fires. The bullet flies through the air just at the moment Polly opens the box. The angel swiftly wields his golden sword and strikes it down in front of her just as the bullet is about to impact, causing it to ricochet off the sword and into the portal as Polly opens the box.

The temperature drops as the room metamorphoses into one large glacier as the portal freezes over and the angel's wings crack and break, causing him to crash to the ground, taking Charity with him. No one can move as their bodies freeze in time although their eyes and minds watch in terror at the being that slowly emerges from within this tiny wooden box. It grows bigger and bigger as it slithers into the air until it towers above them. It's a man, but not human. He's made of ice. They can see through him as his body has no substance, yet the evil pouring out is so pungent that if they weren't motionless with fear and cold it would overwhelm them completely. His face is the colour of clear blue ice and his eyes are cold, so very dark and cold. Droplets of ice trickle from them until they shatter into tiny pieces on the floor. They gather together, forming smaller identical copies of this dark entity, creating a protective shield. His body is a magnificent cut diamond, which glistens and sparkles yet is cold and unforgiving. There is no doubting that this presence is evil personified.

'I am he that is called ICE-OLATION and whoever is touched by my tears of ice will know the emptiness of eternal isolation. Look through my body and see emptiness for I have no heart or soul as neither can live in a body made of ice. I am the bringer of emptiness. I am the bringer of nothingness. Feel the coldness of my tears and know who you are.'

His voice is cold and empty. He has no emotion and can feel no joy or pain. He's incapable of love or hate. He feeds upon the soullessness of others, who as he touches them with his tears become his tears and his eternal servant. They'll never feel or know love again. They'll never know pain or sorrow again. They'll never, ever feel anything again. This will be their fate until the grim reaper taps them on the shoulder and their bodies are his for all eternity.

He looks down upon these mortals and into their souls to see who has been 'marked' to be his servant. He passes Charity for he knows the fire within her soul would melt his tears. He comes to Hilary whose eyes are crazed with fear as he looks through her frozen body into her soul and sees the 'mark'. Two tear drops flow from his dark, cold and lifeless eyes as they roll along the floor until they stop at her feet. She's unable to move or speak as her eyes watch in terror as the teardrops roll slowly up her legs and along her body until they reach her face. They're so cold, like frozen droplets of icy fire, which burn into her skin, leaving tiny potholes as they finally reach their destination – the corners of each eye. No one can save her as everyone watches, helpless and speechless; their bodies frozen in time as the tears of ice disappear into her eyes and a curtain of darkness draws over them.

Another two teardrops appear as his eyes stop before her father, Roland, who has the 'mark' and once again the journey of the tears of ice begins as he too feels the burning fire of their coldness. He looks down upon Polly, whose heart is broken but not cold, her soul still in the light where his 'mark' is unable to penetrate. He needs three souls before his appetite is satisfied, but there are no more 'marks' (a black diamond) in the souls of these wretched creatures before him. But his hunger will not be abated, as he looks deep into the empty shell of his new servants to seek a third. The teardrops appear, only this time they're airborne as they fly through the ship searching for their host. They fly quicker than the speed of light and colder than cubes of ice until they stop outside the cabin door of Vera Uppingham.

They hover, searching for a way in as she sleeps, unaware of her fate, while icy cold liquid seeps under the door emerging inside and reforming into the deadly droplets of tears. She tosses and turns as the tears rest on her pale lifeless face, burning into her skin. She awakes in terrifying pain to feel them penetrate into the corners of her eyes. The veil of darkness crosses her sight and for a second she sees the long cold emptiness of her life flash before her, but she's unable to cry or shed any tears for she feels nothing.

Now he can rest as his appetite, for the moment, has been satisfied. Feelings return as bodies slowly come back to life and Charity regains her voice.

'Who sent you and why?'

'You ask questions when there are no answers. No one sends me, I come when the mark of the black spirit calls.'

'You lie, we come from another time where these souls didn't belong. You entered the box of Thor, which only the power of the Dark One, your master, could penetrate.'

The room explodes with his anger! 'I am no one's servant. I am he that commands and all that I touch is mine.'

'I repeat, your words are false. The power of Thor is mightier than yours and only, Lucifer, the Lord of Darkness, would dare enter his box and send his servant to do his bidding. Speak the truth or Thor will destroy you.'

He laughs aloud, but it is a fearful laugh for he knows what she says is true, yet if he tells her why, his master will reap his punishment.

'My deed is done and the three souls have been "marked" so my Lord will protect me and the power of Thor is useless against him.'

With those fateful words the portal reawakens with a vengeance as the flames of Thor melt its frozen door, restarting the clock of time as the burning arrows of Thor burst through, striking into the centre of the icy cold entity known as ICE-OLATION. Everyone watches spellbound while his screams of horror and pain echo around the room as he and his army of protectors melt into a pool of steamy warm water.

The Captain, his men and the General, swiftly followed by Hilary and her father, rush forward to grab Polly and Charity, but Thor's golden angel regains his power as his wings metamorphose into magnificent feathers of fire, which encircle Charity and Polly, protecting them. The Captain and his men fight desperately to break through as the General and others look on, but the heat is too intense and they can only watch in despair as Polly throws Charity the box and she's carried back into the portal by her protector, Thor's golden angel. They disappear into the closing portal as the flames of Thor slowly burn out, leaving Polly alone, petrified, as she sees her enemies coming towards her. Hilary's bullet suddenly reappears from within the portal as it flies past Charity's cheek, seeking out Polly like a missile. Polly looks at Charity with pleading eyes as she smiles back, knowing what her fate will be.

10

Amnesia

The bullet penetrates Polly's right eye as everyone looks on in horror, waiting for the inevitable, but nothing happens. There's no blood, exploding brain or dead body, just Polly standing there seemingly unaffected. The portal closes and the Captain grabs her arm, while Hilary waits in trepidation, but not for herself. Oddly, she feels strangely calm, almost as if she's devoid of any feelings or emotion. She knows Polly can implicate her but somehow she's fearless. In fact she feels absolutely nothing.

'Polly Melrose, you're under arrest for the murder of Harold Uppingham and Elsie Pritchard. What have you to say to these charges?' says the Captain.

Uppingham waits for her answer, perplexed by his own lack of feelings towards the woman who supposedly murdered his son. Why doesn't he feel anger and hatred? Why doesn't he want to see her destroyed? Why, even though he knows he loved his son, is he strangely detached and unable to mourn his loss? Why does he feel so empty?

Polly stares at all the strange faces peering at her while the Captain's voice melts into her mind, a jumble of meaningless words that she can't comprehend. She suddenly feels very frightened as she looks around. Who are these people and where is she? Who is this Polly? Who is she?

Nothing makes sense. She feels so alone and yet somehow free.

'Who are you? Who am I? Where am I?'

'You know who you are and what you've done. You killed my beautiful Elsie and now you must pay,' the General yells, his whole body seething with anger and shaking uncontrollably, desperate for a drink to take the demon shakes away.

Polly stares blankly at him, unaffected by his and the Captain's accusations. She's detached from reality, her mind and body floating in another dimension. She's in a world, which doesn't belong to any time, a safe world of her own, where reality blends into the dream. It's a warm, colourless place where names, places and people are shadowy illusions. What is her name? She tries and tries but it doesn't come. She feels empty and yet comforted and protected by this darkness that's surrounded her in its protective cocoon of nothingness.

'I...' She hesitates, searching for a name that doesn't exist. 'I don't have a name.'

'Your name is Polly Melrose and you worked for the Uppinghams as their maid and were the secret lover of their son, Harold. Don't you remember?' asks the Captain, already realising that something supernatural has over-taken Polly for how else can he justify a bullet entering her eye and yet her body remains intact. Today he has seen things that no man can explain or comprehend. Dark forces have entered his ship and he's powerless to fight them. He has weapons and bombs, but nothing can destroy what he and his men have encountered today. How can he explain this to his commander? He fears the loss of his ship and his men more than bringing Harold and Elsie's killers to justice. His life is the HMS *Emperor*, he has no family or wife, just the *Emperor*, and she's everything to him. Lose her and his life is meaningless.

130

Polly looks at him like an innocent child whose mind has not yet been touched by the evil of mankind. She desperately tries to think as she contorts her face in agonising bewilderment, yet there's nothing, just a jumble of visions that don't make sense. Dark shapes that look like people, but they have no substance or names. They want something and are tearing at her to get it, but she doesn't have it. Its floats around her, a thin white piece of paper with black letters that, no matter how she tries, is a puzzle that she's unable to unravel as it disappears into its secret place. A place she can't see yet feels she knows. Instinctively she senses that if these dark shapes unravel the black letters then she's no more. The visions and voices tell her to be watchful, but of what? Then the answer comes. Everyone's a suspect, so no one must know, then she'll be safe. That's it!

'I'll tell them nothing,' she quietly thinks to herself, as suddenly her fear disappears along with the dark visions.

'Yes, I know now, blank I be and blank I remain,' she repeats over and over as she retreats deeper and deeper within herself. 'I'm invisible. I have no name. I'm blank,' she replies, smiling innocently as her voice changes from that of a bright vibrant young woman to a secretive child locked in a dark playroom where only the one with the password has the key to unlock it and set her free.

'Rubbish, you killed my brother and stole the list. Where's the list?' Hilary shouts, greedy to get her hands on the six account numbers containing the £2 million. She wants that list. It's hers. She killed for it and it belongs to her, not Polly. Her father looks at her as he begins to wonder if she's told the whole truth. Their eyes meet and for a brief moment their souls are locked together as they glimpse their future; a dark empty place. They don't speak as emotion is replaced by survival. He won't betray her, nor she him, and so the Uppingham

131

name remains intact. Silently they make this pact, which will ultimately destroy them.

Polly smiles, childlike, as she plays in a world of her own, while they all stare, guiltily; at the pitiful creature she's become, knowing that the truth may never be revealed. The 'bullet of fire' has destroyed the woman, leaving an empty shell.

How can they charge her with murder when there's no weapon or bodies and only Hilary's word of a crime, which even her own father distrusts? How can they explain the six people who disappeared through a porthole that wasn't real? How can they explain a golden angel with wings of fire and a dark entity made of ice?

Hilary realises that Polly must remain free if she's to discover where Harold's list is and her father must protect his daughter in order to protect himself. The Captain must protect his ship and his men, and the General, well in the years that follow his drunken ramblings will tell of today's events, but no one will believe him. So at thirty minutes past midnight in the ammunition locker an agreement was sealed that no murders were committed aboard the HMS *Emperor* on **21st June 1940**. Two bodies were washed overboard in a terrible accident, which was witnessed by Hilary, her father, the Captain and his men. Harold and Elsie fell to their deaths while kissing in their secret hiding place, the lifeboats. Polly will remain aboard ship until it returns to England where she will be placed in care and the truth locked inside with her. As this agreement is struck each knows that one day they will pay a heavy price for the betrayal of Polly, incarcerated in an institution for the rest of her life as the real killer or killers go unpunished.

The Captain makes his way back to his cabin to write up the events in his log, while his men escort Polly to her new accommodation, the brig, where she'll be guarded

24-7 and examined by the ship's doctor who'll pronounce her 'mentally unstable', and so begins Polly's journey into oblivion where her only comfort is amnesia, for without memory there's no pain or sorrow, just blankness. The General crawls into his bottle, weeping for his adopted daughter, Elsie, and his own cowardliness at not bringing her killers to justice. Hilary and Roland complete the circle of deception when Vera's grief for her son turns to greed for the money as Hilary finally tells them of Harold's list and the £2 million hidden in a web of secret accounts. The three 'marked souls' that'll spend a lifetime searching for six numbers and whose greed will be the only legacy that they'll pass down to the next generation. The Uppingham dynasty, whose children's children will inherit the curse of the 'black diamond'. Who'll carry the 'mark' that'll separate them from their fellow man, amoral and emotionless, whose sole purpose is to persecute Polly in their search for the hidden £2 million – their inheritance by right of murder.

11

The Source

'Thank God you're safe, we thought the portal had closed and I'd lost you forever,' Monty shouts in a broken voice, trying to hold back his tears of fear. He grabs Charity in his arms as she's carried through the closing portal into the garden by her golden angel before he flies back through the void into the kingdom of Thor.

'Nearly, honey, nearly, but Thor's burning arrows saved me and ICE-OLATION is now a pool of steaming water; so much for Lucifer's dark entity.' she replies, grinning to herself as a dark presence whispers angrily in the wind while they make their way back into the house.

'What about Polly? What happened to her?' Robyn asks as Aunt Lizzy makes tea and everyone sits wistfully around the kitchen table secretly thankful that their journey into the past is over. Sam rings Leo who's so overjoyed to hear her voice that he leaps out of bed (it's one in the morning) and rushes out of the house in his pyjamas. Monty and Jack are a little peeved that they didn't get to experience more of the war, but somehow sense that their journey into the past isn't over yet.

'Polly's safe, but her life, sadly, will not be as others. She was spared prison only to live her life in a series of institutions. Thor's "bullet of fire" saved her from the Uppinghams, but at a heavy price.'

'What price?'

'Her mind, Sam, her mind; the bullet stole her memory and hid it deep in the darkest corners of her mind along with Harold's list where the Uppinghams wouldn't find it. So she lived, but in essence was only a shell whose body died along with Elsie's when Harold killed her and Hilary failed to push her overboard, killing him instead.'

'What a bitch! What a family! Why aren't their souls burning in hell with Harold? Why were they allowed into the Middle Life?'

'The Angel of Judgement will pass sentence, Sam, and until then we must wait.'

'You're safe, you're home!' Leo says breathlessly as he rushes in, crushing Sam in his arms as everyone giggles.

'Darling, you really must do something about your dress sense, it's so urban,' quips Sam.

'Ooooooh urban.'

Everyone jokes as it suddenly dawns on him that he's driven across London in his pyjamas, while they all collapse into hysterical laughter as they relay their story, leaving Leo puzzled.

'How does this help Polly, for we sort of know her secret and why she lost her mind but the whereabouts of the list is still locked inside her memory and the Uppinghams can't have just forgotten about her and the two million pounds over the past sixty-five years.'

'Exactly, Leo, there's still something wrong,' Charity says, interrupting. 'The story didn't end on the HMS *Emperor* in 1940, and our quest for the truth isn't over yet. Polly went from a vibrant young woman to a mental patient in an institution and finally a bag lady living rough on the streets. Why did she have to hide amongst the "living dead" on the streets when she was safe in the institution? Why was she still afraid even though the Uppinghams and Hilary died before her?'

Jack and Monty come alive again as they realise more dark deeds are yet to be uncovered in the mysterious life of Polly Melrose.

'The children, my darling. The children.'

'What children, Lizzy?'

'The children of the children, Robyn, my darling; greed is like a poisonous flower that grows with every passing season. Feed and water it and it'll continue to grow until it devours even the mother that nourishes it.'

'The descendents of the Uppinghams; you're right, Spud, it isn't over yet, the past still hides dark secrets and we're going to find them out,' says Monty.

'But how? We can't use the portal again and time's running out for Polly.'

'I know, Jack, but there are other ways to seek out the spirits of the past.'

'What spirits?' Monty asks, all ears.

'There's a spirit whose soul's been forgotten.'

'I know, I know, it's Elsie's spirit, isn't it?' screams Robyn excitedly, anxious to learn more.

'She can tell us but only if I can bring her soul back from the shadowy world of abandoned spirits.'

'I remember hearing stories of this world as a child,' says Robyn. 'It frightened me as it was a bleak place where spirits go whose souls are so sad that they sink into a pit of despair that engulfs them until they're swallowed up into its darkness. It is said that the spirits who end up there never escape, for their souls are so tortured they don't have the will to come back.'

Leo can feel his stomach churning and his throat drying at the thought of entering this dark world of abandoned spirits. 'I don't like the sound of this. It's dangerous. You're asking the RING to travel back in time and enter this evil place that apparently feeds on souls. What's to stop it feeding on ours?' Charity looks at him and smiles

136

as the rest are quiet – even Jack and Monty, who are the 'toughies' of the group, suddenly feel hesitant.

'Don't worry, Leo, this is a journey only I will make and only souls that are sad remain there.'

'Alone, did I just hear you say the word alone?'

'Don't start panicking, honey, it's quite safe, I'm going to bring the world to me through the cards; trust me, I know what I'm doing.'

'I've heard that one before and there's nothing safe about the spirit world, it's more unpredictable than a woman,' says Monty as Jack laughs aloud in agreement.

'Oh so you think that's funny, the confirmed bachelor who's had about as much experience of women as I have had of army life,' snaps Charity, slightly annoyed at Jack's flippancy.

Jack squirms in his seat as he feels the sharp side of Charity's tongue, while Monty knows his wife all too well and the game she's playing.

'Don't try and make us feel guilty so that you can go off and play the heroine on your own. Leo's right, you're entering unknown territory and in war, if you don't know your enemy, he wins.'

'Honey, I know you speak from a place of love, but when it comes to the spirits only an inceptor has the power to fight that battle. Remember, I have the power of the angels behind me and they'll protect me as they've always done, so stop worrying and let me do what I must do.'

The atmosphere's tense as Charity has her way and Monty concedes as usual, for he knows better than to stop her when she's on a quest. He can't be angry with her for long as there's always this nagging fear inside that one day she'll lose her battle with the dark side and her mortal enemy, Lucifer, will win. How would he feel then if the last words spoken between them were in anger? No, he'd rather lose her to the spirits than lose her love; that he couldn't live with. Charity looks at the pain on his face and knows she's pushed him too far. She, too, secretly fears that one day the dark side will take her, as it once did her father, and she'll be parted from Monty forever; she trapped in the demon world of the Lord of Darkness and he in the light of the afterlife. If this is to be her destiny then at least they will have this time and no words of anger must spoil it.

'You're right, honey, I'm being foolish. I need my family around me and so, if you're all willing, I'll summon Elsie from the world of abandoned spirits with the RING as my protector. You'll form the circle of light that'll keep out the demons and warlocks sent by Lucifer, who'll seize this chance to destroy me.'

'What's different about this time?' Leo asks as Monty sighs with relief. The others, though fearful, don't flinch in their determination to protect her; the RING, that which can't be broken or destroyed by any mortal or spirit when their love is pure, stands resolute.

'Because I'll be opening the gateway to the dark side of the spirit world and awakening Lucifer's evil demons and spirits whose sole purpose is to destroy me.'

'Hmmmm don't worry, honey, I'll be safe alone!' says Monty, raising his eyebrows as Charity grins sheepishly knowing that she sort of deceived him with the 'I'm totally in control' bit. Meanwhile Robyn can barely contain her excitement at watching her mentor at work.

'What cards will you use to bring Elsie back?' she asks, soaking everything up like a sponge so that one day she too will be as great an inceptor as Charity.

'The Source.'

'The Source,' shrieks Robyn with nervous anticipation. 'Oh my God, the oracle cards of light and dark.'

Sam looks at Leo as they both feel that sudden adrenalin of sheer fear race through their bodies.

'What's the "Source"?' Sam asks, screwing her face in tortured anticipation of the answer as Charity contemplates her reply. Should she be gentle and tell her dear friends the simple explanation or go for the full-blown history of the Source? Looking at the pained expressions on their faces she opts for the simple version.

'The Source was once a great monk called Yinnang, who lived in the Tibetan mountains many centuries ago in a time when warlords were fighting imperial emperors for control of kingdoms and so would seek his wisdom before going into battle. He had the power to see into the souls of man and the wisdom to choose which were dark and which were pure. Those who sought his counsel wanted to know how to destroy their enemies, but only those who were pure of heart were allowed to see his visions. Legend has it that there was an evil warlord named Ranghin, who sought his counsel in his desire to rule over all, but was turned away. His anger was so unquenchable that he sent his army to burn the monastery to the ground, killing every monk except Yinnang. He had him brought to his palace where he promised to spare his life if he showed him how to defeat his enemies. Yinnang agreed and allowed him to see his destiny, but what he saw was not victory over his enemies but death at the hands of his own generals. They could no longer watch as their men were slaughtered in their thousands in one bloody battle after another spanning twenty years of barbaric bloodshed in Ranghin's desire to be master of all. So enraged was he by Yinnang's vision that he had all his generals' heads cut off by their own men as an example of his ultimate power and then promoted the executioners. He then ordered Yinnang to be tied to a stake in the centre of his courtyard above a large pit full of poisonous snakes. Every man, woman and child in his kingdom was summoned to watch Yinnang slowly

139

die in agony as the snakes crawled up from the pit and slithered over his body, biting into his flesh with their venom. First his body was paralysed as the venom raced through his bloodstream, causing his muscles to seize up in agonising spasms, while the snakes tore at his flesh, devouring him piece by piece until only his bones remained. It took two days and two nights for him to die as Ranghin's men and subjects watched. This was his way of defying Yinnang's vision of his destiny.

'Did it work, was Ranghin's destiny changed?' Jack asks as everyone sits, visualising Charity's grim 'simple version' of the Source.

'No. Twenty years to the day, at the same time as Ranghin ordered Yinnang to be tied to the stake, his generals crept into the palace and slit his throat with a samurai sword; the very same generals that he had promoted. You see, he never saw the faces of his assassins in Yinnang's vision, only their uniforms, so slaughtered the wrong generals.'

'Well, slaughtering them all didn't alter anything.'

'Consequences, Jack, every action has a consequence, that's how destinies are decided. Sometimes we know the consequences of our actions, but mostly we don't. Ranghin's soul was dark, ruled by greed and rage, which blinded him from seeing the truth. Yinnang knew this and so allowed him to see his future, knowing that the consequences of his own actions would ultimately destroy him.'

'How did Yinnang become the Source?' Monty asks, intrigued.

'When he showed Ranghin his destiny, he also sealed his own, which was sent to him in a vision by his own master when he was only ten years old. He already knew his own mortality and that he would die at the hands of Ranghin, but out of that death he would become immortal. His bones were carried deep into the earth by the very serpents that devoured him, where they remain, protected by the spirits of the serpents, who when resurrected by the oracle cards of light and dark, rise up into the Source, which can then summon the serpents of the past.'

Charity prepares to summon the Source as the RING follows her instructions to the letter, while secretly dreading what's coming next. As they're all seated in a circle in the middle of the large hallway, Charity returns with the oracle cards (given to her by a monk in Tibet many years ago during her travels), and places them in the centre of a large circle drawn on the floor in white chalk by Monty. The circle is divided into five sections; one middle and four quarters. In the middle she places **card one**: The Sun – pure energy, the card that'll summon the Source. **Card two**: Aloneness – a dark sad figure epitomising all the abandoned souls. **Card three**: Innocence – blankness, the beginning of innocence and the resurrection of Elsie's lost soul. **Card four**: Patience, the spirit of time. **Card five:** Past lives – serpents of the past.

Everyone sits in deadly silence, waiting.

'No matter what happens, you mustn't break the RING. Lucifer's servants will try to get into the circle; don't let them in. Once they're inside they'll use the power of the Source to bring forth their master. As long as they remain outside they're powerless, remember, keep your hands locked together and know that your power is stronger than theirs. Light will triumph over dark as long as you remain true to each other. The power of the Ring is impenetrable, even by the Lord of Darkness, as long as you believe in each other.'

Charity stops for a second and looks around slowly, smiling at each of them before asking, 'Are you ready?'

They all take a deep breath, lock hands and say a quiet prayer before replying, 'We are.'

Charity closes her eyes and it begins... She centres

141

her body by performing the chakras, while concentrating all her energies on card **one**: The Sun, which comes alive. It's no longer a tarot card, but a burning circle of pure energy that slowly rises up into the centre of the room; a fusion of gold and red flames emitting such heat that the RING can barely breathe with its intensity. They daren't look upon it for fear of going blind. Within the centre of this burning mass of heat is a dark vortex, which is the gateway to the world of abandoned spirits, but first the Source must be resurrected as the darkness becomes light and Yinnang rises from the earth in the form of a magnificent skeletal python with a human head. He slithers from within the vortex into the centre of the RING, rising up until he towers over them.

'Lord, oh Lord, it must be at least ten feet tall and look at that monstrous head stuck upon those bones, its hideous,' cries Aunt Lizzy.

'It's magnificent,' yells Robyn, 'look how its body moves like a treacherous reptile yet its head is that of an old man, which I swear keeps changing from python to man and man to python. I should feel afraid yet somehow I'm not; in fact I feel strangely drawn to it.'

'I know, I feel exactly the same, it's as if I'm being mesmerised and my body's no longer mine,' Jack says, feeling very uneasy at not being in total control.

'Who awakens me from the earth?'

Its voice is deep and forceful yet the wisdom flows effortlessly from every word as the python asks the question, but the old man awaits the answer.

'I do. I seek your counsel and wisdom, Yinnang, but need your power to evoke a soul from the world of abandoned spirits.'

'What is it that you seek from this one soul that you're prepared to risk losing seven to the darkness?'

'I seek to save the soul of another and return the

142

abandoned soul to the light. I seek your counsel in returning to the past in search of the truth in order to save these souls, and your wisdom in our quest for justice.'

It turns its head, slithering down towards Charity until they're eye to eye. The python runs its slippery forked tongue over her face, while the others watch, clutching their hands tightly, not to keep the evil demons and spirits out but from terror at what's inside. Suddenly Yinnang, the old man, returns.

'I see your soul is pure and your quest is true and I shall allow you into the world of abandoned spirits, but take care, for I've the power to open and close the vortex and show you the way, but not to protect you once inside. Falter in your quest and you may pay the price of all those souls who seek the light only to be destroyed by the darkness.'

He spins faster and faster as the python metamorphoses into a dark world filled with black skies and earth that cries of abandonment and aloneness. The RING is drawn into this world and they struggle to keep the circle intact as the darkness calls to them. An old man in ragged brown robes, carrying a black staff with a python's head upon it, appears as he walks from the darkness towards Charity.

'Whose spirit do you seek and why?'

'I seek Elsie Pritchard and justice for her betrayers and peace for her soul.'

The old man raises his staff into the darkness and calls to the spirits who cry out in despair. The RING hear their pitiful sounds screeching through their ears. The staff melts into a shadowy figure of a woman as she's slowly resurrected from the earth until the spirit of Elsie stands before them.

'Who are you and why have you summoned me?'

'I am Charity Holmes, the Inceptor and I've been

chosen to redeem your soul and save that of another. Justice at last will be yours, Elsie, let me help you back into the light.'

'I don't know you but know that I deserve to be here; I betrayed the General and my country and this is my punishment.'

Sam finds herself shouting, 'You know me, Elsie, remember, you helped Lizzy and me copy the list and saved our jobs and I promised that one day, if ever you needed our help, we'd be there for you, well today is the day. You've paid dearly for your sins, death and sixty-five years of darkness is penance enough, it's time to forgive yourself and do right by another who needs you now.'

Elsie stares at Sam and for a moment she's back on the HMS *Emperor*, 65 years ago, when betrayal and murder sealed her destiny in the darkness. Can she at last redeem herself and feel peace?

'Who needs me and why?'

'Polly, you remember her; Harold's other lover whose soul now hangs in the balance and whose fate could be that of yours.'

Elsie is taken aback by the name of her rival and the reason for her descent into darkness. 'Why should I help the woman who stole my man and my future? Why be so cruel as to ask this of me?'

'Because she's a victim like you and has paid a terrible price for loving a man whose heart was cold and words were false. Now her soul will be lost unless the truth is known and those who truly deserve to be punished remain untouched. Help Polly and redemption and justice will finally be yours and your soul will be free. Help us Elsie, please,' begs Sam as Charity and the rest wait. The cries of the spirits grow darker and more possessed with each passing minute. Time is against them and if they don't

144

leave this evil place soon their souls will be swallowed up and lost forever.

'What is it that you want of me?'

'We need to travel back in time in search of the remaining Uppingham dynasty that inherited the curse of the "black diamond" and have persecuted Polly in their relentless search of the list and the missing millions,' says Charity.

She looks through Charity knowing that her answer will test even the most courageous. 'Only Patience, the spirit of Time has the power to resurrect the serpents of the past, but if I summon her she'll want a soul for the visions that she'll bring. Whose soul shall she take? Who's prepared to pay the ultimate price to save another?'

Monty feels his heart stop and his body crumble as Jack tightens his grip, trying to hold his friend together as Charity replies, 'The charge is mine and therefore I alone am responsible.'

The RING almost breaks as their bodies feel sick with grief and fear at the thought of losing her. Even Leo, who's never been this involved in a case before, feels shocked at the willingness of Charity to give her soul so selflessly so that Polly's may be saved.

Elsie smiles as she moves into the fourth quarter of the circle where the oracle card, Patience, was placed and then turns facing Charity as her body returns to ashes and disintegrates into the ground. The earth beneath cracks open bringing forth a beautiful goddess with long flowing hair made of grass and flowers that cascade down her back and into the soil, creating a mystical garden around her. Her face and body is pure porcelain, perfect, ageless and timeless; for the spirit of Time never grows old. She remains the same, patiently waiting through the darkness of time for the souls who feed her immortality and beauty. Above her head float four white circles, each a window into the past, which will only open to those who've paid her price, their soul.

'Who wishes to seek answers to the past?' Her voice is cold, as is her porcelain skin to the touch.

'I, Charity Holmes, the Inceptor, seek your visions into the past and I'm prepared to forfeit my soul in return.'

'You are indeed a brave, if not foolish woman, Charity. To give a soul for a mere glimpse into the past is a very high price to pay, which once given cannot be undone. Do you still wish to seal this agreement?'

Charity looks over at Monty whose eyes betray his fear, but whose love goes beyond mere mortal understanding. He fell in love with an inceptor and that means he must let her choose her own destiny even if it means he loses her. The RING knows this and so they try to stay strong and keep the circle intact, while inside they struggle to deal with their own torn emotions.

'I do.'

'The agreement is sealed, but the price has already been paid.'

'What do you mean already been paid?' Charity asks, suddenly feeling very afraid.

'The soul of Elsie Pritchard is now mine. She gave it willingly in place of yours. I asked only to see if your soul was pure. My beauty and immortality survive on purity; Elsie gave with a pure soul to save yours and you were prepared to do the same to save another.'

'But I've lost Elsie's, what good is it to save one if I lose another?'

'Elsie's soul was a tortured one as she longed for beauty and love and attained neither. Now she'll know the immortality of pure beauty. Her soul now lives within mine and her ugliness is no longer. She's happy and gave herself willingly to help you, but not totally selflessly, as she desired beauty more than peace. Now I give you the

146

four windows of vision; the first three offer a glimpse into the past and the fourth summons the serpent's eye, which allows the past into the present and so enters your world. But be warned! When you summon the serpent's eye he brings the evil demons and spirits that feed on the souls, which live within it. Their appetite is unquenchable and their desire for fresh blood relentless, and only those who are truly pure of heart will survive the serpent's eye. When you look into the eye of the serpent you'll see all the souls that dared to enter, but never returned.'

Once again Charity and the RING feel a torrent of emotions; relief that her soul remains intact but sadness at the loss of Elsie's, quickly followed by the overwhelming feeling of terror at entering the serpent's eye.

'If the four windows of vision are within the circle then we're not protected,' replies Charity, afraid, not for herself but for Monty and the others.

The goddess Patience raises her perfect white hands up into the dark skies and the four windows part, moving outside the circle, each floating above the clock of time: noon (the serpent's eye), 3 p.m., 6 p.m. and 9 p.m.

'The clock of time begins at the third hour with each window allowing you three hours in mortal time to look into the past and seek the answers to your questions. Once the third hour is struck, and no matter where you are in the timelessness of the past, one window closes and the next opens until you reach the twelfth hour and the serpent's eye, where the final vision will be the most treacherous and maybe your last!'

Then, as instantly as she appeared, she returns to the earth, which swallows her up, leaving behind a single patch of grass in the centre of the circle from which a tiny root penetrates, growing rapidly and ferociously until it's taller than man, as it takes on the form of a living wand with green shoots sprouting from its tip. It bends and turns with the flexibility of putty but has the strength of steel running through it as it contorts its way towards the first window, 3 p.m., and touches it with its tip, leaving behind one single green shoot. It returns to the centre of the circle, standing erect, while the green shoot disappears into the window, revealing the first vision.

It's 1960 and the RING watch as Roland Uppingham lies on his deathbed, aged 70, while Vera and Hilary stand stone-faced and emotionless, waiting, as he slowly slips into the dark jaws of death. Beside them is Father Jacobs, performing the last rites, while downstairs in the mourning room sit Hilary's children, fathered by a man whose identity and whereabouts is unknown. These are Roland's grandchildren: Victor and Jean, twins aged ten years. Hilary and Harold reincarnated; their likeness sends a shiver down the spines of the RING. Their souls bare the mark of the black diamond and the curse of the Uppingham dynasty. They sit calmly and coldly, waiting, not to hear news of the death of their beloved grandfather, but of the list and their inheritance. Will he reveal any secrets that'll lead them closer to the £2 million? Or will he die taking those secrets with him?

Roland opens his eyes and looks upon his wife and daughter; their faces are lined and marked with the ravages of time; a time that hasn't been kind to either. Vera, now 68 and withered, with a sharp pale face and deep set lines portraying the hardness of a woman with a dark soul. Hilary, who's grown more embittered and callous as the years have passed in her relentless persecution of Polly. She's 45 but her body, heart and soul is that of a haggard old witch, which as each year passes leaps into old age faster than the lives of a cat whose seven years span but one. Roland's thin, watery lips rub together as air and bubbles evaporate from his mouth, while saliva trickles down his chin as he attempts to speak. Vera and

Hilary bend closer as Father Jacobs prepares to anoint him while he whispers in that frail final voice of death.

'I see the black spirit of death, he comes for me. I'm lost.'

Hilary's anger erupts as she sees her last chance slip away with his dying breath.

'But the list, father, do you see the list?'

He looks at the cold eyes of his once beloved daughter and a teardrop trickles down his sallow, grey face; the first tear to be shed since that fateful day 20 years ago on the battleship HMS *Emperor*, when his soul was marked by the evil entity ICE-OLATION. For a brief moment he remembers what it's like to feel love, the love for his lost daughter, and then the pain of emptiness when love is replaced by greed and avarice. 'Forget the list, daughter. It draws you closer to the dark side where he's waiting...'

'Who's waiting? Father, father, do you see the list?' Hilary screams, shaking him viciously as Vera just watches. Father Jacobs looks on in horror as Roland Uppingham gasps his last breath and slips into the shadows of death.

'I'm afraid he's gone, Miss Uppingham,' says Father Jacobs sympathetically, trying to pull her back as he anoints him on the forehead before reciting the final prayer.

Vera and Hilary stand frozen as they look down upon the frail, lifeless body of their once proud and righteous husband and father. They shed not one single tear for their loss, just the callous frustration of two cold and embittered women unable to extract the last drop of knowledge needed to get them closer to the list. Father Jacobs tries to offer words of comfort but they mean nothing to these two mercenary women. He leaves them to their grief! The door closes and suddenly they feel the shadow of death creep over them as they look behind to see it coming. It seeps through the walls and creeps along the floor, a black spiritless entity searching for its soul; the one that bares the 'mark'. They watch, cold and detached, seemingly unaware of their own fates, as it slithers onto the bed and slowly devours its prey until it reaches his head. He opens his eyes and they see his terror and hear his final cry of despair as he's swallowed up into the black bottomless pit of tortured souls, who languish unloved and unwanted in the darkest corners of the 'Middle Life', where despair triumphs over hope.

Everything goes black as the RING feel themselves drawn back into the circle, where the wand moves towards 6 p.m. and the next vision of time.

It's seven years later, 1967. The black spirit of death once again comes to collect what's due. Vera, now a frail 75-year-old, lies in the very same bed that claimed her husband, who had looked up at her while she watched, callously, without love or compassion, as the dark side of the spirit world claimed him. Now it's her turn, as she lies there, helpless, feeling for the first time in 27 years what fear and abandonment are. Not for her the hand of a loving daughter to grip for comfort and strength in her final hours, but a sea of detached, embittered stone faces. Hilary, 52, who bears the mark of a haunted spirit, a spirit that never knows peace, is with Victor and Jean, who've grown into their mother's likeness, but without the burden of ever knowing what love is. Since their birth 17 years ago they live for only one thing: their inheritance, and they'll stop at nothing to get it. Father Jacobs again prepares to send another into the afterlife, but this time he offers no words of comfort to her or the family, for in the seven years that have passed, the Uppingham reputation has surpassed even his ability to turn the other cheek. They've become relentless in their desire for power and status, using any means necessary to obtain the riches that they perceive as their birthright.

Anyone or anything that stops them taking what they desire is destroyed and many a life has fallen into the pit of despair as they take and take until there's nothing left. They live a rich life in a grand house, which has been obtained through the blood of others. Their name is spoken of with hate and terror, for cross the Uppinghams and it's the last thing you'll do. No longer a respectable family working for the bank, but money lenders who pray on other people's sorrow like leeches, sucking the very life from their hosts. They own properties, businesses and people, but still it's not enough; they want more. But the one thing they've never been able to own is Polly, who still eludes them, but they're closing in and her time is running out.

Vera calls to Hilary who once again bends over the dying body of a parent, but still she feels nothing except the cold shiver of the spirit of death drawing closer, but not to collect her mother. This spirit is for her and for a brief moment she's face to face with her own mortality, where the world that awaits her is not the comfortable one she's destroyed so many lives to obtain, but a dark, evil place. A whisper passes her ear.

'Oh the sweet pain of death and the eternal torture of darkness. Soon, Hilary, soon you'll be reunited with your loved ones, for all eternity.'

She leaps back as the twins and Father Jacobs see her fear.

'What is it, mother? What did she say?' Jean asks sharply, not out of concern for her mother, but simply to hear news of the list and her inheritance.

'Nothing, it's nothing,' she replies, pulling herself together; again she bends down to hear her mother's dying words.

'Polly's brain, take her brain and the list will be yours.'

Vera joins her husband and the two are reunited, but

151

without love. Not for her an eternity of peace with her loved ones; instead a unity sealed by the blood and despair of others, which will torture them with their cries of anger and hate for all eternity. What price now would they give to undo what has been done in the name of greed. All that glitters is not gold, but a brightness that quickly succumbs to the dark when the flame burns out.

Once again Father Jacobs sends another Uppingham into the darkness of death, while the ones that remain behind give little time to grieving. Again his words of comfort fall on deaf ears, as unlike the last time, no one waits behind and Vera is left alone to face the black spirit of death as her family rush downstairs to discuss her dying words and the 'clue' that'll draw them closer to the list.

Time runs out and the window closes as the vision of the Uppinghams disappears, leaving the RING waiting, while the wand moves to the third window: 9 p.m.

The clock of time ticks on and the RING find themselves in England in 1987 where the family are gathered at the funeral of Hilary, who passed away a week ago aged 72. How quickly those 47 years have gone when, as a young woman, she destroyed the lives of Harold, Elsie and Polly through her jealousy, and crossed over to the dark side, sealing her fate with the demon devil, Lucifer, who patiently waits in the Dark Life, where there is no time; just eternity. Soon the **Angel of Judgement** will seal their destiny, and Hilary, together with her parents, will know their final fate, redemption or to join Harold in the Dark Life, where their souls will burn for all eternity.

While Father Jacobs, now a frail old man, recites the familiar prayers of death, he glances at the Uppingham dynasty. Victor and Jean, now in their 37th year and the beneficiaries of the Uppingham empire, which has become so powerful that nothing is beyond their reach, except for the one thing that still eludes them, Harold's list and the missing £2 million. They've no need of it but have driven Polly further into the pit of madness in their relentless quest for what they consider their birthright. Standing by Jean is her husband, John, a cruel, secretive man with a paranoid personality who sees everyone as an enemy. He married her for money and power and uses them both viciously on anyone who crosses him. No matter how they begin, friend or colleague, they always end up as an enemy to be 'dealt with'. He's five years older, with an evil, sallow face, dark eyes and thin lips. His hair is thinning but spends a fortune on hair transplants, which no one dares mention for fear of retribution. There's no love between them, just the bond of cruelty, which somehow ties them together, as she uses him to torture Polly and he uses her money and power to torture everyone else; a short man with a short fuse but a long, bitter memory.

At their sides are the children, Craig and Alexandra, aged 12, the third set of twins borne into the Uppingham dynasty. Once again Hilary and Harold reincarnated, only with each set of twins their souls grow darker. The black diamonds' poison grows more treacherous with each generation until it tears out the heart, leaving only a black hole, which sucks the life out of anything pure. Like their parents, they're cruel and dark with a manipulative streak, which they use mercilessly to destroy anything or anyone that suits their pleasure. They've no friends and no longer go to school as no one can control them or the evil mind games that they play. No teacher or child in the school wants to know them, they're feared, and so now have a succession of private tutors who last less and less time with each passing year as their evil powers grow stronger. It is said that the Devil is within them and that they revel in it.

Finally, standing alone is Victor, who's never married, preferring the illusionary world of drugs and the endless procession of male lovers, who fill his bed at night when the demon spirits visit, torturing him with visions of his own violent death. When the light of morning comes his need for company and the warmth of a body beside him vanishes only to return again when darkness descends and the nightmares begin. Not for him the loving relationship of a single companion to share his life with, but the paid lover whose only requirement is money and who can be discarded as easily as a piece of merchandise.

The Uppingham dynasty and the curse of the spiritless black diamond that eats away at each generation until there's nothing of humanity left.

As the rain pours and Hilary is buried in the earth her children shed no tears, for love is an emotion that eludes them. Father Jacobs returns to his church and prays for the souls of a family that'll never understand the selflessness of thinking of another. He knows how dark their souls are, but still he prays, hoping against hope that his God will listen and grant them the vision of His light.

While the Father prays for their redemption they continue on their search for Harold's list as they visit Polly in a place called The Willows, which has been her home for the past 20 years. A life spent in institutions; 47 years locked away in a clinical, cold world where the Uppinghams have spent a fortune trying to retrieve another fortune. At 67, Polly is now an old and broken woman with a child's mind, who can no longer remember the laughter and joy of her youth, when she stepped aboard that train 47 years ago and into a future filled with betrayal and nightmares. Never again would she know the love and warmth of her family, who searched in vain for the daughter and sister that disappeared into oblivion. When the Captain handed her over to the doctors all those years ago little did he know what a terrible sentence he had placed upon her. As the years rolled by he often wondered what had become of her, but never went looking for fear of what he might discover. He's long since died, but his soul is restless and wandering in the Middle Life, waiting for her to find peace so that he can finally move into the light of the afterlife.

She looks up from her table in the big white sterile room where all the 'residents' go to sit and watch TV or play games and pretend that their lives have meaning and that somewhere someone cares. The nurses keep watch in their crisp white uniforms, detached and devoid of any feelings as their charges shuffle around, endlessly trying to find a way out of their tortured minds, only to be numbed into nothingness by their daily cocktail of drugs.

'No, no, please not them,' she screams inside her mind as she sees her tormentors staring back at her through the glass partition that separates the mad from the bad! Jean, John, Victor and the twins, who are allowed to come along and watch as they steal her thoughts. Twenty years of torture born out of Vera's dying words, 'Take her brain and the list will be yours'. Those evil grins that she fears so much as she's carried off, screaming, to the 'pain room', where they tie her down with leather straps to a metal bed underneath a piercing white light that blinds her eyes, which are taped back so she can't close them. Above her are the 'white suits', greedy doctors who torture her for money and then punish her again when she reveals nothing. As they strap her in and pump her body full of drugs she can see her defilers looking down from the glass ceiling, smirking in that creepy way, which makes even the doctors shrink with fear. The twins lick their lips in eager anticipation at seeing and hearing her screams, which is all the more delicious when they merge their minds with hers and feel her fear and pain. If only they could see the list, but it's buried too deep, protected by her madness, which somehow senses that should they ever penetrate into the darkness of her inner world it would seal her death.

'I want you to treble the dosage. She's going to give us the information we want and this time we'll not stop until her thoughts are ours,' commands John as the twins feel a surge of excitement, while Jean and Victor let him play his cruel games upon a helpless old woman whose suffering is endless.

'But she's too old and weak to take it any more, it could kill her,' replies one of the doctors as John fixes him with those dark, empty eyes.

'Remove him.' Within seconds John's 'protectors' carry the doctor out, while the others freeze, afraid to say or do anything.

'Get me the information I want or you can join your associate,' he yells as they quickly prepare Polly for the 'mind game'.

The RING hear her screams and watch her body leap on the bed in agonising convulsions each time the electrodes send shock waves of electricity racing into her brain. The twins twitch with sadistic pleasure as they feel her body's descent into violent and agonising despair. They watch the screen to check her brain waves and analyse her thoughts as the computer converts them to words. But still they make no sense, as always, they are the same.

'Blank to blank, turn the key and play with me.'

'What key? Twenty years and always the same riddle, we'll never find the list, it'll go to the grave with her,' shouts Jean as she smashes her fists against the glass. Polly's screams can be heard throughout the hospital corridors and into the wards; even the 'residents' stop and feel her pain.

'Up the dosage again,' shouts John. At this even Victor has a moment of compassion.

'She's too old and her brain's fried, face it, there's nothing there.'

John and the twins look at him, shocked and amazed that he should dare think of defeat and even worse, feel.

One of the doctors suddenly gets an attack of conscience at the thought of actually killing a 'resident', which supersedes his fear of the Uppinghams as he plucks up the courage to say, 'I feel I should point out that if we increase to the final level her heart won't be able to take it and we may lose her.'

'I didn't ask for your opinion, just do it,' he yells, while Jean and Victor suddenly feel afraid, not for poor Polly, but at the thought of losing their inheritance.

'Are you sure we should push it this far, after all she's no good to us dead?' she asks, slightly nervous, as even she knows not to get on the wrong side of him.

'Do you want the bloody list or not?'

'OK, OK, we'll do it your way, but remember, if she dies I want my two million.'

He looks at her coldly as Victor stands silently waiting for the eruption, while the twins revel in their parents' bickering.

'Don't threaten me unless you can back it up.'

As they glare at each other the doctors prepare Polly.

'Well don't just stand there like lemons, get on with it,' shouts John.

Everyone takes a deep breath as the button is pressed and Polly's screams erupt through the hospital like a tornado. Her body reacts so violently that her chest and arms explode, ripping the leather straps from the table, thrusting her into the air as sparks fly from her like deadly arrows, destroying all as the room comes alive with electricity. Machines and people explode as the smell of burning flesh creeps through the walls and their dying screams echo around the hospital, while her torturers look down in detached amusement, safe in their glass fortress.

The emergency bell rings as the hospital staff rush in to find a room filled with charred and burning corpses, exploding machines and the lifeless body of Polly still lying on the bed.

Darkness descends as the clock of time ticks on and the third window of visions closes.

12

The Serpent's Eye

The wand is still as the RING wait, terrified of entering the serpent's eye, but nothing happens.

'Why isn't the wand moving?' Monty asks, anxious to know about Polly, but scared of what demons the serpent will bring.

'Those who summon the serpent's eye must do so willingly otherwise it can't take your soul,' replies Charity as everyone feels sick with fear.

'We have to ask the wand to open the fourth window, which once entered can't be closed until the serpent has had its fill.'

Leo starts shaking. Sam and Robyn forget themselves for a moment and unlock their hands as they cover their mouths, trying to stop themselves from throwing up.

'You mustn't break the power of the Ring,' screams Charity as she loses control for a moment, but already she fears the worst.

'Sorry, sorry we forgot,' cries Robyn as they link hands quickly, hoping that a split second isn't enough time for Lucifer's demons to enter. Besides, they can't see anything, but Charity isn't so sure as her gift begins to sense an entity within the circle, yet she's unable to see what or where it is. If it's already in the circle then it's too late, but until it reveals itself there's no point in scaring the others. Meanwhile Jack is getting restless, as the soldier within him wants to go beyond where the average man would dare venture.

'We've come this far, so we can't turn back now and, besides, we're all pure of heart here, so there shouldn't be a problem, should there?' He looks around at the others who aren't so convinced.

'Well the great Lord himself is our protector and his power is stronger than any snake so let's get on with it,' says Aunt Lizzy sharply, her patience growing thin.

Monty agrees. 'I'm with Jack and Lizzy, we need to know the truth and I hate loose ends.'

Sam and Leo nod their heads somewhat more timidly as Robyn looks across at Charity, sensing her fear that dark forces are already amongst them. They smile at each other, knowing that it's too late and so Charity summons the serpent's eye. She looks to the wand, which appears to look back as it bends towards her, waiting for her command.

'I call upon the eye of the serpent to open the fourth window and bring forth the souls of past lives.'

The wand turns and as it bends and weaves its way to the final window, the RING hold their breath as it leaves behind the last green shoot before disappearing back into the earth.

The temperature drops to freezing as the room descends into darkness and everyone feels their hearts pound in terror as their breaths float in the cold, black air. Above them the window metamorphoses into two enormous black-blue misty eyes in the form of a figure eight, which is held together by two yellow and red-winged serpents sitting beside each other as their claws and fangs lock into the serpent's eyes. They lash their tales back and forth, while hissing and spitting their yellow venom as the eyes begin to open revealing the trapped and tortured

160

souls that dared to think they could enter the eye of the serpent and survive. It's a terrible sight, which sends shudders of fear down the spines of the RING as they witness the torturous screams and cries of thousands of desolate grey spirits floating inside a bubble with no escape. Crushed together like sardines, they scratch and tear at each other while trying to break free, but there's no way out, as the eye of the serpent is impregnable.

Suddenly from within the centre of each eye a dazzling light appears, melting together into a fusion of brilliant yellows, greens, pinks, blues, purples and dark reds, forming a blazing arrow.

'Don't look into the eye of the arrow or blindness will be your destiny,' shouts Charity as the RING avert their gaze from the intensity of its colours. They can barely keep the circle intact as they try to protect their eyes, without unlocking their hands, from the unbearable heat of the flaming arrow as it flies towards them. It stops, dead centre, floating above them as they glimpse from the side of their mind's eye the entity within the flames, a beautiful white light, which slowly transforms into a brilliant white ghostly figure of a naked woman. She's magnificent, a flawless, glorious white light, with a cat-like face, black eyes and a perfect womanly body encased in a fusion of burning colours. She floats within the arrow, protected by its flames, her demeanour so enticing that the RING struggle in their fight not to be drawn into this wondrous world of hers. But Charity knows this spirit, an evil, bloodthirsty serpent, who traps her prey in the illusion of beauty.

'Whatever she says, don't be drawn into her world, it's not real. She's not real. She'll try to entice you with promises of eternal pleasures, but once she's tasted your blood your soul is hers, trapped for all eternity in the serpent's eye, where she feeds on your despair and pain.'

161

'Who wishes to enter the serpent's eye?'

'I do.'

She looks down upon Charity, who averts her gaze, careful not to look into the centre of her eyes, which mesmerise her victims with pleasurable thoughts, drawing them into her world.

'Ah, an inceptor,' she replies in a soft, seductive voice that melts through your mind, seducing you with delicious visions of a magical world full of beautiful mystical spirits whose only wish is to serve you.

'I see you have the power of the angels within you. Why would such a powerful inceptor seek the eye of the serpent when you have the mighty guardian angels to show you the way?'

'I must seek the souls of past lives alone and without interference from my guardians. My quest is for me alone to solve otherwise my charge will be lost. The angels can only watch otherwise justice will be tainted and the truth not pure.'

She looks around at the RING as they succumb to the intensity of her charms, slowly being drawn into her world.

'Don't look at her and keep your hands locked, remember she's not real, just an illusion of your desires. She feeds off of your thoughts; don't let her in,' Charity urges as they bring themselves back from the brink of dreams and into the reality of the serpent's pit. She smiles, knowing that her price must be paid if she's to bring the souls of the past into the present.

'You know you must relinquish a soul for a soul and I see you seek more than one,' she replies, licking her lips in anticipation of all the souls she sees before her.

Charity pauses, trying desperately to think of a way to enter the eye without giving her their souls. 'I seek only one soul, that of Polly Melrose.'

She laughs aloud as she flies through the air, swooning

in and around the circle and the RING, as the flaming arrow's rainbow of colours lights up the room taking their bodies into immeasurable pleasures, while they battle to stop themselves following her into the serpent's eye, which waits patiently. As they watch the arrow they're drawn towards the eye as it transfigures into a magical world filled with sparkling stars and happy laughing spirits protected by two magnificent white unicorns. Oh how enticing it looks and how much the RING desire the pleasures of this wondrous world.

'You can't have them,' yells Charity, as she feels her family drifting towards the eye.

'I seek only Polly Melrose, one soul only.'

'To find the answers you seek I must summon all the souls that surround the past of your charge; a soul for a soul, no less no more, but payment must be made.'

Charity feels her strength ebbing away as the serpent's eye draws closer and closer and the RING grows weaker and weaker, until the eye is over them, ready to take its fill.

'Stop, stop. I'll give you a greater prize than these mere mortals,' Charity screams.

The eye retracts as the entity returns; her lips are wet in anticipation of this 'prize'.

'Hmm, you intrigue me. What have you to offer in place of your souls?'

'Lucifer's High Priestess of Secrets.'

'You dare to insult me. I could devour you all now for such stupidity,' she screeches, her voice no longer the sweet, alluring temptress, but the snake she really is. But Charity stands strong as the RING hold on, weak and afraid, as the magical world of the unicorn fades and the dark world of the serpent's eye returns.

'I speak the truth, the mistress of the Lord of Darkness is amongst us, sent by him to destroy me. She possesses

163

all the secrets of the undead, whose souls languish within her dark spirit, still alive in their mortal bodies; the undead, who are darker and more evil than any grey soul. Destroy her and you'll possess all that was hers and your powers will be infinite.'

'If she's here, why doesn't she reveal herself and how did she enter the circle without my knowing?'

'The power of the RING broke momentarily, allowing her entry where her presence grows stronger as she waits within its shadow to see if I succumb to the serpent's eye. Destroy the eye, her protector, and she will be revealed.'

'You try to trick me into destroying the eye to save your friends and gain entry into the past without paying, knowing that once the serpent's eye is vanquished I no longer exist.'

'If you are destroyed I lose the link to the past and any hope of saving my charge, but if you destroy Lucifer's dark angel, the High Priestess of Secrets, then both our destinies will be fulfilled. You have the power to destroy her and possess all of her secrets together with the power of the undead, is this not worth more than our feeble souls?'

'Your reputation is well deserved. You offer me the ultimate prize that you know I'll be unable to resist; the prize that'll save your friends and gain you entry into the past, while destroying both your enemies in one stroke. I destroy Lucifer's mistress, taking her powers, but incurring his wrath and possibly my own destruction. What a dilemma I find myself in and yet the thought of having infinite powers is too alluring to refuse; the temptress finally succumbing to temptation. Very well, Charity, I accept your prize.'

She turns to face the serpent's eye and looks into its heart and all the souls that are trapped within it as their screams fill her with delight. For a moment Charity fears that she'll not be willing to let them go, but then it begins.

The beautiful white vision transforms into a blazing arrow as her face melts into the tip and she flies towards the eye, a burning flame of fire. It strikes into the centre, destroying all as the eye and the screaming souls trapped within explode into grey particles of burning flesh, while the eye's protectors, the winged serpents, spread their wings and take flight only to be caught within her flames, melting into white ash. The serpent's eye is no more. Charity and the RING watch, frozen in fear, as the battle between Lucifer's dark angel, the High Priestess of Secrets and the evil serpent spirit begins.

With her protector gone she's revealed, a beautiful beguiling moon goddess holding her scrolls of secrets and dressed in a queen's fine robes of pale blue and black silk with a brilliant white lunar disk upon her head, the crown of the Queen of Darkness. Floating behind her is the Black Curtain of Knowledge, which holds all the secrets of the undead, while at her feet is a crescent moon that is said to contain the power of Lucifer. She is the link between the dark underworld of her Lord and the mortal world, where she collects the souls of the undead and traps them for all eternity behind the curtain. Once she has their soul, their names are written indelibly in the scrolls of secrets, which are the centre of her power. It is said that the one who possesses the scrolls can claim the infinite powers of the High Priestess and rule over the demon world of the undead, who exist only to serve the one who possesses their souls.

'You seek to save yourself, Charity, by using the serpent spirit, but no spirit is powerful enough to defeat me. Soon all your names, including the serpent's, will be written within my scrolls and the dark world of the undead will be your eternal destiny.'

165

Her voice is cold and lifeless. Charity and the RING feel her evil presence all around them, as they desperately try to cling onto each other for strength. She looks down upon her victims, counting the souls that'll soon be hers, while the serpent spirit reappears again in womanly form. They lock into each other's gaze, their eyes dark and empty, but both confident that they'll be the only 'one'.

'You dare to challenge me, the Queen of the Undead, and mistress of the great Lord Lucifer. Surrender now and I'll be merciful and let you keep your pitiful existence, for I have come to collect another soul today.'

They glare at each other as the serpent spirit ponders her offer, which is generous indeed and not one to be taken lightly from such a powerful dark angel. But her desire to possess all the scrolls' secrets and be mistress of the undead is too great a temptation. She hisses and spits her poisonous venom towards her enemy, the High Priestess, while her body shape-shifts into a hideous black serpent with blood red wings as she grows taller and taller until she towers over all that's before her. Her teeth drip with poisonous saliva as her long black tongue attempts to wrap the priestess in its powerful grip, while trying to squeeze the life force from her. As the serpent's tongue curls around the priestess she spreads her magnificent red wings and flies closer, feeling confident that victory will soon be hers.

The priestess doesn't flinch as the serpent's tongue crushes her body, while she sinks her teeth deep into her flesh, injecting the poison that would kill a mortal within seconds. Charity and the RING watch in terror as the evil serpent hovers over its prey, flapping her huge red wings back and forth as her gigantic head tears into the priestess's flesh, drawing blood. She hisses with delight as she thinks to herself how easy this has been and soon the scrolls will be hers.

166

But just at the moment she smells victory, darkness descends. The crescent moon metamorphoses into a demon vampire bat, whose wings span the entire room as it flies straight towards the she serpent, sinking its teeth into her head. She screams in agony as the vampire tears away at her scaly flesh until she's dripping in her own blood and eventually forced to let go of the priestess, who tumbles to the ground as the scrolls fall from her hands, landing beside Charity, who picks them up before the priestess can reclaim them. The serpent and vampire tear at each other until the room is awash with their flesh and blood. They screech and scream as, piece by piece, they rip the flesh off each other until only bone is left and their battered and torn wings struggle to maintain flight. The High Priestess watches as her protector and the serpent destroy each other until all that remains is their bones, which crumble to the ground, where the earth swallows them up.

The priestess rises up until she's floating high in the air, but her powers have diminished as she's without Lucifer's crescent moon, and her scrolls are in the hands of her enemy, Charity, who knows the power she now possesses.

'I can still destroy you, Charity, even though you have the power of the scrolls, but I wish to have them returned so what is your price?' she asks, somewhat more penitently.

Charity knows this dark angel can't be trusted, and once she has the scrolls back she'll destroy them all in the name of her master, Lucifer, who she fears more than the power of the undead, which can be released by whoever holds the scrolls. She must be more devious than the priestess if she's to destroy her and find a way back into the past now that the serpent's eye and its spirit has been vanquished.

'I wish only to discover the secret of my charge's past

and so need to travel back to the last window of visions and the year 1987.'

The priestess sees her chance to regain the scrolls and the power of the undead, which once in her possession, she'll use to carry out her master's bidding.

Charity allows her to see her vulnerability, knowing that, even without her scrolls, the priestess's ego wouldn't contemplate defeat by a mere inceptor. She draws her in with her pleas for help, knowing that these will ultimately be her undoing.

'If you bring forth the past and grant this wish then I will return the scrolls to their rightful master.'

'Give me the scrolls first and then I'll grant your wish.'

'I may not posses the great powers of such a magnificent dark angel, but I'm not as stupid as to give you your infinite powers back without my wish being granted first.'

'How do I know that once I open the final window of visions you'll release the scrolls to me?'

Charity must be very clever if she's to outwit this mighty dark angel and not only save herself and the RING, but destroy the priestess and gain access to the past without leaving the present.

'You have the power to call upon the Angel of Completion, who has the gift of 'dark sight', who'll grant us both completion.'

The priestess ponders for a moment, wondering why Charity has made such a request, knowing that the Angel of Completion has utter contempt for inceptors, who she sees as inferior, whose gift of 'sight' is a mere shadow of her powerful dark sight, and who takes great pleasure in destroying any inceptor who crosses her path.

'If I bring forth the Angel of Completion she'll seek to destroy you. Why do you risk this for an old woman who means nothing to anyone?'

'She's my charge and I'm sworn to help her and fear

not the Angel of Completion as long as I hold the scrolls, which I can use to destroy you both. But I'm not a dark angel and seek only the truth. Therefore once you grant me my wish I will give the scrolls to their true master, who'll protect me from the "dark sight" and release you from your burden of powerlessness.'

Charity knows that her last words will cut through the Priestess's soul, for if there's one thing she fears more than her master, Lucifer, it is being powerless. She needs the scrolls to regain her status as Lucifer's most powerful dark angel.

'I'm their true master and I could use them to destroy you once in my possession, so why do you trust me so, Charity?'

'I trust the power of the scrolls which I'll call upon for protection before I release them and which must obey the master that holds them.'

'You are indeed cleverer than I gave you credit for. I resurrect the Angel of Completion to grant your wish that's then destroyed by me in return for the scrolls, who you call upon for protection. Everyone wins except the Angel of the Dark Sight, who's expendable. I like your proposal; it is one that is worthy of the darkest of angels, who I'm sure one day will be your ultimate destiny.'

The priestess raises her hands and removes her crown, which holds the power of the Queen of Darkness within the disk and places it upon her thrown as it rises up from beneath the fires of hell. She places her right hand upon the white lunar disk, while reciting the demonic words of her dark Lord, Lucifer.

'Demonicadracula, Demon of the Dark Sight, rise up and bring forth the knowledge of completion. I, the High Priestess of Secrets, summon you, Demonicadracula, the spirit of the dark to show yourself.'

Darkness closes in as the room becomes smaller until

it's no bigger than a black box. The lunar disk grows larger as the smell of evil chokes in the throats of Charity and the RING, who grip onto each other tighter than ever before.

The disk floats above them as they feel trapped in the tiny black box, while the priestess sits on her thrown outside looking all powerful as cracks appear within the disk. They spread rapidly, forming a jigsaw puzzle, which when complete becomes the face of an angelic child. It looks so beautiful and innocent as it glows bright like the moon, but as Charity and the RING look closer they see in the centre of its forehead that a piece of the jigsaw is missing. Slowly it opens its eyes to reveal nothing but blackness; the power of the Angel of the Dark Sight has been awakened.

'Who dares awaken me from my sleep?' it yells angrily as Charity and the RING recoil in fear at the mighty roar that leaps from its angelic lips.

'I, Lucifer's High Priestess of Secrets, have summoned you to grant a wish to my servant, Charity, who seeks the knowledge of the past.'

The child looks at the priestess, who's holding her crown minus the disk and knows that unless she grants her wish the disk will not be able to return to its resting place. She looks down at Charity and sees that she's an inceptor, which does not please her, knowing that she must help the very vermin that she despises.

'So you seek my help, the great inceptor, whose powers are so inadequate that you're unable to help your charge without calling upon me.'

Charity knows that she mustn't upset this powerful dark angel, who could destroy them with one blink of her dark eyes, yet she's aware that while the priestess holds the crown she rules over her.

'I'm your servant and wish only to help my charge and

realise that it is only by your good grace that my quest for the truth and completion for my client will be granted. I beg you to grant me this wish and know that the High priestess of Secrets will reward you well for this service.'

'An inceptor who knows her place, how refreshing,' she replies arrogantly. 'I see you wish to return to the year 1987 when your charge disappeared from the last window of visions. Very well, I shall grant you your wish, for today my spirit is light and I'm feeling generous towards my inferiors.'

Her eyes grow wider until Charity and the RING are staring into the abyss of darkness, which gradually draws them in until they're inside the missing piece of the jigsaw: the fourth and final window of visions where they return to the year 1987.

The Willows is alive with the flames of hell as the staff and patients screams of despair float in the black air and the hospital crumbles to the ground, leaving behind mound upon mound of black ash. Charity, Monty and the others walk through the ash as it burns through the soles of their feet, holding their breath to protect themselves from the stench of burning flesh where the spirits of the dead remain. They hear the pitiful cries of the spirits who languish forgotten and forsaken; cries that ring out through the thick black mist of death that surrounds the empty shell of the Willows.

'All those poor souls burned alive with no one to hear their cries for help. How could such a terrible thing happen? Why weren't they saved? Sometimes even I can't understand how our Lord can allow such atrocities. Why didn't he save them? Why, my Lord? Why?' cries Aunt Lizzy as the tears flow down her cheeks. The others can barely contain their grief for the death of so many innocents.

'I know, Lizzy, sometimes God seems a cruel and unforgiving Lord, but he isn't a destroyer of lives; he gives life and the price of life is sometimes death.'

'Well, bully for him, so he doesn't actually kill anybody, he just lets people kill each other as he watches from his throne high above, doing nothing,' snaps Robyn as she struggles, along with the others, to understand how life can be taken so easily and with such callous regard.

Charity doesn't answer, for even she can hardly believe that the death of so many can be regarded as the 'Will of God'. Surely life is precious and therefore worth more than the fate of these poor souls. They continue on their journey through the ash and crumbling walls of the hospital until they arrive at the room where it all ended, as they stand motionless and weary. Suddenly a dark vortex comes spiralling towards them until they're standing at the edge of a black oasis of nothingness; the fourth and final window of visions.

They see the bodies before them, some still just recognizable, while others are just bone and ash, as the staff come rushing in. Above, looking down from their cracked glass fortress, are the instigators of this barbaric and brutal crime, the Uppinghams, who watch coldly and without remorse as the few remaining hospital staff collect the pitiful burned corpses, placing them one by one in rows until the full horror of their crime is laid before them. Body upon body of innocent souls burned alive in their unrelenting search for their 'inheritance'. Not a single tear is shed, just detached annoyance at still being no closer to the whereabouts of Harold's list.

Victor and Jean stare stone-faced as the realisation suddenly hits them that they've lost the last link to the £2 million and Polly, whose lifeless body is still lying on the bed that was used to torture her. John and the twins revel in the blood and death of so many; John with that dark smirk of his and the twins soaking up every last drop of death and despair as they feel the pain of each soul wandering helplessly in the darkness of the Middle Life, searching for peace in the spirit world.

They feel the ground beneath move as the cracks grow bigger and the fortress begins to crumble. 'We're done here,' says John coldly as he and the twins make their way towards the door.

'Well that's just great. You kill Polly and lose our inheritance and all you have to say is "we're done here",' screams Jean as Victor remains still and silent, afraid to encounter John's wrath, knowing that he could be next in line for a black plastic body bag.

'Shut up, you stupid woman, the old bag was an imbecile who couldn't even remember her own name, and your family hasn't been able to get anything out of that pickled brain of hers for forty-seven years. I didn't lose your inheritance; it was lost years ago when a bullet destroyed her mind. Face it, my dear, you've been chasing a lost cause for the last forty-seven years and I've just put that pathetic old witch out of her misery and saved you from wasting any more time searching for fool's gold.'

Their eyes penetrate each other, locked in pure hatred, neither willing to admit defeat as the twins hold hands and smirk, relishing every bitter word spoken by their 'loving parents'. Meanwhile, Victor feels strangely drawn to Polly's body, which seems to be calling to him.

'Blank to blank, turn the key and play with me. I win, I win, you lose, you lose.'

'Did you hear that? She's still alive?'

'Hear what?' John asks angrily as he pushes past in a hurry to leave.

'Polly, she's not dead, I've just heard her voice taunting me.'

'Don't be ridiculous,' replies John as they all look down

173

at Polly's body, which is strangely unmarked and intact. She lies pale and lifeless on the table with a big grin on her face. They continue to stare; it's obvious she's dead yet somehow her body still feels 'alive' and is taunting them with that grin.

Suddenly they feel very uncomfortable; even the twins are nervous, as the tables are turned and Polly becomes the torturer instead of the victim.

'Get rid of that body. Bury her separately from the others and make sure the grave is deep,' shouts John as the staff look up shocked at the coldness he displays towards the victims.

'But we have to perform a post-mortem,' replies a nurse angrily.

He looks directly into her eyes as she feels the fear racing through her body. This is not a man to argue with. 'What did you say?'

'Ugh, nothing, sir, except where would you suggest we bury her?'

'Don't bother me with such trivialities, just make sure she's buried deep. Put her in the hospital incinerator for all I care, in fact that's not a bad idea. Yes, that saves you digging a hole, burn her.'

Everyone's speechless, even Victor and Jean feel bad. For in their own way they'd become attached to Polly over the years with their monthly visits to 'pick her brains', which, as the years rolled on, became more of a game that filled their otherwise empty lives. Somewhere deep down inside they secretly admired this frail old lady, who no matter what tortures they performed upon her, never revealed the secrets locked inside her head.

'Sometimes I wonder what I ever saw in you,' says Jean, surprised at her own feelings of sympathy towards Polly.

'Look in the mirror, my dear, and the answer is there,' he replies as they leave their glass fortress just as part of

174

the floor collapses to the ground almost killing yet another 'disposable member of the human race'.

Polly's body is bagged and tagged as she's wheeled away to the boiler room in the basement, which has escaped the perils of the fire, but where ironically she'll burn in the furnace until her body is nothing but white ash after miraculously surviving intact when all others were reduced to bone and ash. She's left on the trolley in the boiler room as the nurse searches for the porter to dispose of her remains, while the rest of the hospital is in chaos dealing with the aftermath of the fire. There she lays, her frail 67-year-old lifeless body finally at peace, smiling, as she's no longer at the mercy of the Uppinghams.

Eventually the nurse returns with the porter and gives him his instructions before leaving Polly to her fate. He turns his back on her as he opens the doors to the furnace, pumping up the fire in preparation to receive its 'guest', while the heat intensifies and the sweat beads drip from his forehead onto the floor. He checks the thermostat, tapping it to make sure the 'old girl' is working to full capacity before turning back to find, no corpse! Just an empty trolley. He scratches his head in bewilderment as he desperately searches for her body in and outside the boiler room to discover nothing.

He's in a conundrum; does he tell his bosses that a corpse has just got up and walked away, which they won't believe, or does he keep quiet and mark his records as tag no. 45 burned to ash in the boiler. The latter appears the better option as the fourth and final window of visions closes, leaving Charity and the others even more perplexed than ever.

If Polly died in 1987 aged 67 then who is the old woman who sought out Charity's help 18 years later aged 85, and where did Polly's corpse go?

175

13

The Fallacious Spirit

Suddenly they're back in the present, trapped in the black box as the Angel of Completion floats above with the missing piece of jigsaw in the center of its forehead, now completed. The High priestess sits on her thrown above them all waiting to redeem her scrolls, enabling her to destroy her enemies.

'I don't understand, if Polly's dead then who's the old woman?' Sam asks as Monty and Jack look around nervously, realising that there's no way out of the black box and that they're all at the mercy of the two dark angels above. Meanwhile, Charity's brain is trying to fathom the mystery of Polly's missing corpse.

'Yeah, whose soul are we saving then?' Robyn asks, while Leo and Aunt Lizzy slowly cotton on to the fact that Monty and Jack are worried. They all gradually realise that they're trapped in the Angel of Completion's black box.

'The scrolls; give them to me, Charity, for I've completed my part of the bargain,' demands the priestess as everyone waits, anxiously, wondering how they're going to escape from the box intact.

'What about my prize? I've done your bidding, priestess, and the souls within the box are mine. Release them to me,' demands the Angel of Completion impatiently.

The priestess turns, her eyes dark with anger. 'How dare you demand anything, you are my servant and do my bidding. The souls in the box are mine.'

Suddenly she realises what she's said as she looks down upon Charity, who knows this evil dark angel will destroy them all once she possesses the scrolls. Instantly the priestess rises up from her throne, wrapping herself within her robes of silk, which suddenly transmute into a gigantic black scorpion with an enormous tail that expands and grows as it curls up and around its body, wending its way towards Charity, its tip swelling with poison.

'Oh my God, we're finished,' cries Leo as everyone looks on, helplessly, while the tail of the black scorpion gets ready to strike at its prey, Charity. She looks straight into its vile black eyes as the Angel of Completion watches, knowing that once the black scorpion of death has tasted blood then its appetite becomes unquenchable until all that surrounds it has succumbed to its sting.

'Use the power of the sacred scrolls, quickly before it strikes,' yells the Angel of Completion, suddenly feeling incredibly protective towards the very inceptor, who just a few moments ago it was seeking to destroy.

Charity unfolds the scrolls, thrusting them into the air, forming a barrier between her and the scorpion's tail. Its poisonous tip strikes at the scrolls, which come alive with the flames of the angels of fire, who fly out from within the sacred parchment pages. Four angels whose entire bodies are alive with the flames of the souls of the undead, who come forth to protect the rightful master of the scrolls, Charity. For it was written within the secrets of the scrolls that only the one with the power of the angels of light could release the souls of the undead, bringing forth the angels of fire. They fly up and around the scorpion, breathing their red flames of death upon it as its scaly black body combusts into thousands of pieces of charred flesh, which fall from the air like black raindrops of death as the RING frantically brushes them off until all that remains is a black heap of dead scorpion flesh spread on the floor of the box.

The angels then turn and fly towards the other dark entity who feeds off the souls of the dead, the Angel of Completion, who suddenly needs the help of the inceptor it despises.

'Charity, you must stop them. I helped you, now you must help me.'

Charity looks up from the box, knowing that this dark angel is at her mercy as she calls upon the angels of fire to stop. They fly within inches of the luminous face of this angelic but evil child of the dark sight, expanding their wings of fire as they float in front of its terrified eyes, waiting for the command of their master.

'If I allow you to live then you must release us from the black box and every other soul that you have captured in your quest for the power of the Dark Sight.'

'But if I release them then I'm vanquished, for it's the souls of the dead that feed my infinite powers of sight, giving me immortality.'

Charity looks up at this angelic jigsaw face of a child, which without its arrogance suddenly appears fragile and lonely, a child in need of a mother's love.

'Trust in me and do this one good deed and not only will all the souls you've trapped be released but also you'll bask in the power of the angels of light. Believe in them and the power of the scrolls and they'll show you the power of luminous sight and you'll become the Angel of True Sight; your ultimate destiny.'

What to do? If this dark angel doesn't release Charity and the RING then the angels of fire will destroy it, but can she be trusted? Are Charity's words true or false?

There's no way out for this evil entity as Charity has outsmarted both dark angels.

Suddenly the room grows bigger and brighter, while the box slowly disappears, leaving them back in the safety of 29 Chalfont Square. The Angel of Completion has released them and awaits its fate, hoping that Charity's words are true as she holds the power of the scrolls in her hands, commanding the angels of fire, who hover above, resplendent in their flames of death.

She looks up into the face of this now conquered and beaten dark angel, saying, 'Thank you. But now you must release the souls of the undead and then the power of true sight will be yours.'

Once again this dark angel must trust in an inceptor, which in the past, it took pleasure in destroying and to whom it has never shown any mercy. Will Charity finally have her revenge for all her sisters that it destroyed or will she show the mercy it never did? Again it has no choice as it feels the burning flames of the angels of fire, who hover dangerously close to its now melting face.

It closes its dark eyes and opens its mouth as the souls of the undead fly out in their hundreds, white luminous spirits crying with tears of joy as they're freed from an eternity in the Dark Life. They swoop in around Charity, brushing against her body as they whisper their gratitude, offering her their eternal protection from the evil demons and spirits of the dark life before disappearing through the walls into the afterlife.

Charity looks up and into the face of this dark angel, which no longer has the power of the dark sight in its eyes as the darkness disappears, leaving two hollow and empty holes. The luminous light begins to fade, as does the jigsaw puzzle, leaving a white void of emptiness. The evil Angel of Completion is no more and its powers of the dark sight evaporated, leaving it at the mercy of its enemy, Charity.

Once again she raises the scrolls into the air and commands the angels of fire to return to the sacred parchment as the scrolls mutate into a giant wing of fire, which flies up into the angels' disintegrating face. The power of the angels of light glows within it as it slowly transforms into a beautiful burning globe of the world encased in a protective circle of human spirits that emit the light of luminous sight. It's reborn into the Angel of True Sight as its face appears within the globe, smiling at Charity as their eyes lock and the bond of everlasting friendship is sealed before it disappears into the ground, leaving behind a single red disk the size of a 50p piece. As Charity bends down to pick it up, she sees the globe in miniature at the end of a rope made up of its protectors: the human spirits.

'What is it?' asks Monty as she places it around her neck.

'Something that one day I'll need,' she replies as they all wearily wend their way into the lounge, collapsing into the safety of the mortal world.

Drinks flow glass after glass as they regain their composure. Even Jack and Monty sink more than their fare share of double whiskies, while they contemplate what might have been.

'Next time I agree to visit the spirit world, stop me, please!' bemoans Sam as she clings onto Leo, who's never downed so many spirits in one go.

There follows a long period of silence as everyone tries to fathom the mystery of Polly, her missing corpse and the old bag lady who purported to be her spirit in form of the **patient**. Who was she and how was she connected to Polly? What happened to the last decendents of the Uppingham dynasty? Where are they today and did they finally find Harold's list and claim their inheritance? What did the final words of the **patient** really mean when she charged Charity with the quest to give her back her name?

'They want what I know, but I was too clever for them and made myself invisible. Everyone knows me, but no one knows me, as I'm invisible. I was too clever for them and they'll never find it now. I win, I win, they lose, they lose. How clever I've been, my dear, but you know, don't you, don't you.'

They're back to square one, only now they're even more disarranged than ever and still no closer to saving their charge, who they're not even certain is Polly Melrose. Time is running out as the **15th August** draws closer when the Court of Past Souls sits again and the **Angel of Judgment** passes sentence.

'I can't believe we've gone through all of this to find that we're still no closer to discovering the identity of the **old woman**,' moans Robyn, infuriated that they appear to have been manipulated by a frail 85-year-old ghost.

Charity smiles that little grin of hers, which Monty knows so well.

'I know that look, Spud, don't keep us in suspense. Who is the **Patient**?'

Everyone looks to Charity, whose silence exudes an eerie menace that shudders through their bodies like the cold wind of death before answering, 'She's a **fallacious spirit**.'

14

Mephistopheles

'What kind of spirit? I've never heard you mention its name before and why has it chosen to seek you out in this elaborate way?' Robyn asks, suddenly feeling very frightened as her gift of sight sees into Charity's mind and knows that this spirit is malevolent, bringing with it the vilest of messages: death.

Charity braces herself as she explains. 'It's a false spirit sent to deceive and lure its victims into its world where, eventually, it takes possession.'

Everyone sits up, their eyes darting everywhere. Aunt Lizzy holds her sacred cross close to her chest, while Monty's usual composure descends into dark fear as he realises that the forces of evil have been with them every second since Charity's first meeting with the **patient**. They've been playing with them, watching and waiting, but always one step ahead. Even now they're in the room, feeling their fear and laughing at them as they watch and wait until they're ready to strike.

'I don't understand, do you mean that everything we uncovered wasn't real, the people, the places, the past, the secrets, that it's all been an elaborate illusion, a lie?' cries Sam, holding Leo's hand tightly as they all feel each other's fear, which even the intrepid Jack and normally cool Monty can no longer hide.

'Yes and no,' replies Charity as Jack asks nervously:

'What do you mean, Miss Charity, have we been investigating an illusion?'

Charity breathes deeply before beginning. 'The best lies are born out of truth, and the **fallacious spirit** is a master in the art of dissimulation. Everything that we've seen and experienced is "real" in that the people, the places the secrets and the past existed and happened in the way that we were shown. That is the **truth**. The **lie** is the illusion behind the **truth**. A dark and evil spirit has been sent in the guise of **truth** hidden in the illusion of a **lie** so that we can't see what is real and what is false until, eventually, we're defeated. Then and only then will He come to claim what is His.'

'You're frightening me now, Spud,' Monty interrupts. 'If he is who I think you mean then he's been with us all the time, taunting us, playing a game, but all the while holding all the cards. He wins and we lose. How clever he's been. He made himself invisible through the illusion of the **patient** knowing that you would come to her aid. You know him so well and yet you didn't see who he was until now when it's too late. He wins, he wins, we lose, we lose. How clever he's been.'

'Oh my God, I see it now, the Court of Past Souls isn't sitting in judgement of Polly, but Charity,' yells Robyn as it all suddenly becomes clear.

'What do you mean in judgement of Charity?' whispers Aunt Lizzy, her voice shaking as she feels her heart beat faster and the beads of fear for her beloved 'daughter' trickling down her now pale and horrified face.

Charity can feel her pain, but she must be strong otherwise all will be lost, for she needs the strength of her friends and family more than ever. The RING must be united if she's to defeat her arch enemy, Lucifer, the supremely evil one, sometimes known as Mephistopheles.

'You see, Lizzy, my dearest, if I fail to discover the **truth** behind the **lie** and where the real spirit of Polly is then I fail to give her back her name.'

'But I still don't understand, my darling. Why would this mean that the **Angel of Judgement** would pass sentence upon you and not Polly?'

'Ah, Lizzy, the world of spirits is not that different from the mortal one in that the spirits that live within that world still possess the same inherent strengths and weaknesses that they had when alive. If they were evil or good in life then they continue to be in death, only there's no escape from their destiny in the spirit world, just an eternity of either pleasure or pain. The **fallacious spirit** is the darkest of spirits who desperately wants to return to its mortal body, to once again feel the pleasures of the human flesh and real blood racing through its veins. It doesn't feel remorse for the sins of its mortal life, instead it wants to relive its life again, but with the powers of the Dark Life bestowed upon it so that it can wreak havoc and mayhem. Sometimes Lucifer will seek out a truly evil spirit, offering it a second chance of mortality but with the power to cause infinite depravity upon earth. Imagine the elixir of reliving your mortal life again, but this time around your powers of inflicting immeasurable pain upon your victims is limitless. This evil spirit becomes the **fallacious spirit**, willing to do Lucifer's bidding in return for his mortality.'

'But I still don't understand, my darling, what has this to do with the **Angel of Judgement**?' interrupts Aunt Lizzy, still confused.

'It means that if I can't draw out Polly's trapped spirit from the illusion of the **fallacious spirit** then he has the right to demand that the **Angel of Judgement** releases Polly's soul in return for mine. Then I become the **judged**. I should never have been deceived by a false spirit, which indicates to the **Angel of Judgement** that there lays within me a seed of evil, whereby he's then duty bound to strip me of my powers as an inceptor. Then **judgement** will be passed upon me for deceiving the court with my claims of pure sight. You see, my dear Lizzy, I then become the **fallacious spirit** in the eyes of the court and so must be sent back to the Dark Life, where Lucifer is waiting. He wins, he wins, I lose, I lose.'

Sam and the others squirm in their seats as they realise how fragile Charity's powers really are and how easily they can be taken, along with her, if Lucifer wins in his quest to claim her soul.

Meanwhile Charity begins to feel the power of Mephistopheles as she succumbs to the thought that maybe there is a dark side to her soul that has yet to be awakened.

'All my life I've fought to save the innocent from evil demons and spirits of the Dark Life and now I discover that this very vileness is within me, waiting to be awakened by its master, who'll call upon it if I don't succeed in my quest to find the real Polly and unlock the key to her mind, releasing her soul and finally giving her back her name.'

Monty erupts in an explosive rage, born out of fear for his beloved Charity, for he's always felt an evil presence floating around her, never tangible but always there, waiting. Even though they've fought so many battles together against the forces of evil sent in different guises by the darkest of fallen angels, Lucifer, he's always felt that somewhere in the lineage of her past darkness was inherent in her family, an evil so abhorrent that even her parents have kept it from her. They protect her more fiercely than a lioness protecting her cubs, but why? Lucifer is relentless in his quest to destroy her and claim her soul. Even when his own children were destroyed at the Final Reckoning their loss meant nothing to him, just seeds of evil propagated to gain power over the mortal world. Yet he can't let go of Charity. Why? What is it that she possesses that he covets so much?

'I won't have you talking like that, Spud. You are the purest of inceptors, untainted by sin and with the protection of the most powerful angel of all. There is no darkness within you, just the frailty of human error, which even you can succumb to.'

She smiles at him, knowing that he feels her fear, but she takes comfort in his words, for there is truth in them. Yes she is the Inceptor, but she's still mortal and therefore doesn't possess the divine sight of her Lord, the One True Being.

'Once again you're right, honey, I've been a simpleton in my trust of a false spirit who's stolen the spirit of an old woman to deceive and destroy me, but I have seen through it and will discover the truth. Polly did seek me out, but was intercepted by the **fallacious spirit** and therefore her soul is still waiting to be redeemed and that is the reality. The Court of Past Souls will sit and we shall destroy the demon that has taken her soul.'

'But how? We've come to an impasse with Polly's death being some eighteen years earlier than we thought. Where do we go from here?' Leo asks, still trying to get his head around who's false and who's real.

Charity laughs aloud as she looks at the pained expression on his face, which as she casts her eye around the room, appears to be cloned on everyone.

'If Polly's spirit wasn't intercepted by Lucifer's evil servant, the **fallacious spirit**, then we would have still made the same journey and found the same clues; it was Polly's spirit calling to me and always has been. So we continue on our quest to discover the true identity of our mysterious **patient** and then present our findings to the court whereby the **fallacious spirit** will be expunged and the real Polly freed.'

Monty isn't comforted by Charity's simple answer. 'But what if we fail, Spud, and don't discover the real Polly in time?'

Everyone suddenly freezes as they look to Charity, who always seems to be left with giving the bad news.

'Then Mephistopheles wins.'

15

The Sign

It's the next day and everyone's subdued at breakfast as they all quietly rack their brains trying to think of a way forward in solving the mystery of Polly Melrose in time to face the court, which is only two days away.

'I wish Himself above would send us a sign. After all he gave you the blessed "gift" or "curse" in the first place and now he's just abandoned you to your fate, Charity, my darling,' snarls Aunt Lizzy, as she stomps around the kitchen scowling and banging crockery.

'That's it! Lizzy, you're magnificent,' screams Charity as she leaps in the air hugging and kissing her soft round face.

'Ah get away with yah, girl, what's all this about?' she asks as her face blushes bright red, while secretly enjoying the affection of her beloved Charity.

'The Angel of Signs, Lizzy, she can show us the way. I don't know why I didn't think of her before,' shrieks Charity as she rushes to her quiet room to fetch the *Sacred Book of Angels* along with her angel oracle cards.

'Clear the table, Lizzy, we're back in the game and this time we're going to win.'

Within no time Aunt Lizzy's cleared and scrubbed the kitchen table ready for Charity as everyone forms the circle round the table to complete the Ring of Power.

'I'm beginning to get the hang of this psychic stuff, in fact it's rather addictive in a strange sort of way,' says Leo, suddenly feeling the adrenalin rushing through him as he watches Sam and the others prepare to enter the world of spirits. Charity carefully places the book on the table next to her cards as Monty and Jack pretend to look cool and in control, while Robyn explains in intricate detail how the *Book of Angels* is used to bring the angel oracle cards to life. For the first time he truly sees why Sam loves her 'adopted family' so much and how the bond between them is so strong that it is indeed an impenetrable RING.

The time has come. Charity sits at the head of the circle. To her left sits Robyn and to her right Monty, her two guardians, while her soldiers, Jack, Aunt Lizzy, Sam and Leo form the ranks. They all join hands, except for Charity, who takes the cards as she prepares to summon the Angel of Signs.

She moves the book into the centre of the table, closed and face up, while placing the pack of 44 cards face down upon it so that all that can be seen is the picture of an angel's gold and blue wings flying, alone, in the timeless space of a pale-blue sky on the back of the cards. Gently, she closes her eyes to perform the chakras as the RING joins hands enforcing the power within the circle. Leo looks around as he feels the atmosphere around him suddenly changing, while Charity's third-eye summons the Angel of Signs.

Suddenly they're surrounded by a blue vortex of universal space, travelling beyond earth's atmosphere heading towards the world of angels. Hundreds of twinkling stars encapsulate them within this whirling vortex, emitting the most beautiful of lights, whose warmth glows within them. Charity opens her eyes to look upon the book and cards as they rise up from the centre of the table, floating

189

within the vortex and encased within a golden ring of light. The angel's wings take flight from the cards until they're floating directly above the RING, magnificent in their splendour as they spread apart to reveal a brilliant blue light, which slowly transforms into the Angel of Signs resplendent in her shimmering blue robes and glorious mane of golden hair.

She looks down upon her subjects and smiles before gently saying, 'You've asked the heavens for a sign, Charity, and my Lord has sent me to deliver it. Pay careful attention to the evidence and trust in your gift.' She raises her right hand and points towards the stars, which join together within the vortex to form an opening that leads to a staircase.

'Climb the staircase of knowledge, Charity, and all will be revealed, but remember, the questions that you ask don't always give the answers that you desire.'

'But where does the staircase lead and how will we get back?' Sam asks as she squeezes Leo's hand tightly.

The angel doesn't answer as she disappears back into the heavens, leaving behind her wings, which return to the cards. The staircase awaits them as they all look to Charity, who once again must lead her family into the abyss of the unknown.

'There doesn't appear to be anything beyond the steps,' comments Sam, still concerned that no one seems to be worried about where they're going and how they're going to get back.

'Don't worry, Sam, the Angel of Signs has shown us the way and we must climb the stairs if we're to discover the truth,' replies Charity as she places her foot on the first step.

'Oh God, oh God, here we go again, stepping into the unknown without a by-your-leave, where evil creatures, demons and spirits in the Dark Life could be waiting,' mumbles Sam under her breath as Robyn gives her a dig with her elbow while frowning at her. Not for her the fear of the unknown, instead she relishes the idea of going beyond the boundaries of her mortal world and into the uncharted sphere of the spirit world.

Finally Charity reaches the top of the staircase with Monty by her side as they look down upon an endless pit of hollow emptiness, which, if they step off the safety of the staircase, could lead them into oblivion.

They lock hands and turn to face each other, smiling, confident in their love before looking back at the others, who even though they're afraid of what lies beyond, do not flinch in their determination to seek the truth as they leap into space.

Their bodies tumble down and down into this never ending pit as the passage of time rushes past and they see themselves from conception to birth; from birth to childhood to adolescence, and finally adulthood. The joy, the laughter, the deaths, the loss, the pain, the struggles and the love that each and every one of them has experienced flashes before them as they rush towards the bottom of the pit. If they were dying then maybe this is what it would be like to see their lives flashing before them...

16

The Spirit of White Silk

All of a sudden they're back in a hospital ward, but not the Willows. The clock on the wall strikes 10 p.m. and the calendar underneath marks the date of the **15th August** in the year **1965**.

'That was some journey and I'm not sure I like seeing my life flashing before me, especially all my mistakes, of which there are many,' jokes Jack as they all nod and laugh in agreement, pulling themselves together, all that is except Charity, who didn't get Jack's joke.

'What do you mean your life flashing before you? I didn't see anything, just lots of dark whirling nothingness,' Charity says as they all look at her in puzzlement.

'You mean to say you didn't see one single element of your life?' Robyn asks, as Monty and the others suddenly feel that cold shiver of doom racing through their bodies.

'No, not a single thing, but then I'm only meant to see other people's lives, not my own,' she replies lightheartedly, but inside that nagging doubt once again rears its ugly head as she contemplates the thought that maybe there is a seed of evil within her, otherwise why would the memories of her life be nothing but darkness?

'Are you OK, Spud?' Monty asks squeezing her arm affectionately, which pulls her back from that dark place that keeps recurring in her thoughts.

192

'Yes, honey, just making sense of where we are,' she replies, as they look around the ward, which is dark and quiet as the patients sleep and the night nurse is sneaking a quick break with her lover, Dr Smyth, in the laundry cupboard.

'Where are we? It doesn't look like the Willows, in fact it's a general ward,' comments Robyn as they tiptoe towards the patients, who all seem to be well out for the count.

'We need to check out the patients because there has to be a reason why the Angel of Signs has sent us here,' says Charity as they split up and take a patient each, reading the nurses' notes at the bottom of the beds.

'Surely be to God this can't be no coincidence,' whispers Aunt Lizzy excitedly.

'What is, Lizzy?' asks Monty in a constrained voice as they all rush to bed number 5, where an elderly man is sleeping.

Lizzy proudly shows them his notes, Mr Parr, suspected heart murmur.

'Well, well, the innocent bank clerk from the Bank of England in 1940,' quips Jack as they suddenly hear coughing from the bed in the corner, which wakes Mr Parr up. They quickly rush to hide behind the screens in bed 7, which is empty. They watch as he sits up and looks around, helping himself to some water, when the patient in bed 10, in the corner, starts ranting.

'Harold, please stop, please leave me alone, I can't remember. Send them away, Harold, please, I don't know anything,' she cries as Mr Parr calls out for the nurse to attend her, but she's busy in the laundry cupboard and so he makes his way over to her as she continues to ramble uncontrollably.

'I don't know where the list is, leave me alone,' she screams, holding her head in her hands as Mr Parr tries to calm her down.

'Who are you talking to, there's no one here?' he asks as she suddenly sits upright in the bed and stares straight at him, saying, 'You know them, I know you know them. Tell them to leave me alone. I can't stand the voices, they won't leave me in peace.'

'Know who? I don't know you,' he replies as he starts to return to his bed.

'No, don't go, don't leave me to them, please help me. I'll tell you if you promise to help me. Please, I just want the voices to go away,' she shouts, grabbing his arm, pulling him down towards her as she whispers in his ear. Charity and the others desperately try to hear what she's saying, but it's no good, she's too far away and they can't risk being seen.

Suddenly Mr Parr stands upright, looking all around, allowing them a glimpse of him from the light shining through the door leading to the corridor. He's a tall thin man with a crooked, almost sinister smile, which seems to be permanently part of his face. It's the smile of a devious and cunning man, who has no morals, yet is fragile, as he knows that death is looming round the corner. He opens the door to the corridor to see if it's empty and then makes sure that everyone's asleep before returning to the woman, who's now lying peacefully. Then, coldly and without hesitation he takes a pillow from underneath her and places it over her face, holding it down firmly, as he slowly takes the life from her before returning calmly to his bed.

'My God, he's just killed her in cold blood,' whispers Leo, shocked to witness an actual murder and angry that he just watched and did nothing.

'You're a witness to the past, Leo, and nothing can change that which has already been.'

Just as the last words trip off Charity's tongue, something appears to be happening to the dead woman as her body

194

takes on a new 'life force'. They see something white pouring out from her mouth; it's fluid yet has substance as it continues to flow from her onto the bed and then the floor. The RING looks on as it begins to form a shape until they see the silhouette of a woman standing by the bed, totally white, but with no features. Yet the body of the murdered woman is still lying on the bed, intact, as her white ghostly apparition stands motionless, waiting.

'Holy mother of God, what kind of thing is that?' Aunt Lizzy whispers, loudly, while frantically making the sign of the cross as the others look on in utter bewilderment.

'It's called ectoplasm, otherwise known as the spirit of white silk,' replies Charity, who has never actually seen one herself as they are extremely rare in the spirit world and only appear in exceptional circumstances. In fact, she's never come across any psychic or spiritualist who's ever witnessed one first hand. This is indeed a rare privilege and a moment that isn't afforded to just anyone.

'So why them and why now?' she wonders.

'This is amazing, I never thought in my wildest dreams that I'd ever actually see the phenomenon know as ectoplasm, yet here we are almost within touching distance,' says Robyn excitedly as Charity tries to calm her down.

'Shush, Robyn, she mustn't see us.'

'Why, what is this so called spirit of white silk?' Monty asks, suddenly realising that although Charity is somewhat mesmerised by this apparition, she is also very afraid. But before she can answer, the door opens and in walks the night nurse who sees the silhouette in the corner.

'Who's there? How did you get in?' she asks as she makes her way over to the ghostly figure. As she gets closer she begins to feel frightened as she realises that something is very wrong. Suddenly, it moves, and within seconds it's devoured her completely into its white silky body until she's gone.

'Jesus, did you see that?' says Jack as the ghost begins to move their way.

'Christ, we're next,' cries Sam as they all freeze and huddle together behind the screen. Suddenly it stops at bed number 5, Mr Parr's, who's also seen everything, but strangely doesn't seem afraid. They watch, shaking, as the ectoplasm mutates into the shape of a woman, the night nurse.

'Thank you, Mr Parr. The contract is sealed and you may collect your fee as agreed.'

He just smiles that crooked grin of his as she walks away, passing bed 7 when, just for a moment, she hesitates before leaving the ward as they all breathe a sigh of relief. After what seems an eternity, Mr Parr slithers back under his bedclothes and goes to sleep as they creep out from behind the screen and tentatively make their way towards the dead patient in the corner bed. As they stare down at her lifeless body they see the pale, spent face of a middle-aged woman, but there's no doubting who she is. Even though time has not been kind, Charity can still see the resemblance of the pretty, dark-haired girl in the locket. Robyn checks her chart at the end of the bed, which simply says, name unknown, address unknown.

'Now I'm totally confused. Here we are looking at another dead body of Polly Melrose, only this time she was murdered in 1965, some twenty-two years previous to her other "death" at the Willows in 1987 and some forty years prior to her "last death". What's going on, Spud, and what was that thing that just walked out of here and what "pact" has Mr Parr made with it?' Monty asks as Jack and the others constantly look behind them in the darkness of the ward, just in case the ectoplasm returns.

196

'We can't discuss it here, but I now see everything clearly and what an evil game our **fallacious spirit** and its conspirator, the **spirit of white silk** have been playing with us.'

'What game?' Sam asks, making sure she's standing well back from the body, as there's no way she's going to get grabbed again by another corpse.

'Don't you recognize the hospital and this ward, Sam? Doesn't it feel strangely familiar to you?' says Charity as Sam slowly looks around, soaking in every detail.

'No it can't be!' she replies as it suddenly dawns on her.

'What can't be?' Jack asks, impatient as ever.

'It's the same ward that I stayed in when I had my operation and Mr Parr's bed is the bed I had ... ugh, just thinking about sleeping in the same bed as that slippery toad makes me ill. And this is the corner bed that our **patient** first called to Charity from. I mean, the layout's the same as in our time, it's just that the décor, technology and patients are different, except for Polly's corpse, which seems to keep dying and disappearing over and over again.'

Everyone is still as they look around the ward, being careful not to completely divert their eyes from the dead body in the bed. Suddenly the door opens and they see the silhouette of a woman coming towards them. But before they can move she's upon them and instantly they know that she is the **spirit of white silk**, as their bodies are glued to the floor with terror...

197

17

Consequences

There it is, floating in front of them, the intoxicating vision of a woman's body encased in pure white liquid silk, which appears to be transmuting constantly between spirit and human form. It hovers just above the floor as it slowly glides around them, leaving a circle of white silk behind, forming a barrier that traps them inside.

'What's it doing?' Robyn asks, suddenly losing all her excitement at seeing this mythical spirit made from ectoplasm, as she now realises that the reason no one ever reports seeing one is that they aren't around long enough to tell anyone.

'It's trapping us in her circle of ectoplasm so that it can eventually steal our essence.'

'I don't quite follow what you mean, Miss Charity? Why does it want our essence, whatever that is?' Jack asks as he feels his body becoming numb, while this thing just floats outside the circle, waiting.

Charity tries to answer, but like Jack and the others, her body is closing down as she feels the heavy weight of death looming within her. 'Ectoplasm isn't a real living spirit, it's an evil entity made out of liquid that is constantly searching for host bodies in which it can feel the pleasures of mortal flesh. But it can only take the essence of your body, leaving your real body in "limbo" until your essence is all used up when it then looks for another host.'

'What happens to the body in limbo?' Robyn asks, struggling to open her mouth as the onset of rigor mortis begins to take hold, even though she's still alive.

'It stays in limbo, doomed to wander forever in the place it was left, unable to move on to the afterlife. It just exists in the empty shell of its dead body where its essence, its very being, its soul has been devoured by that evil floating pile of ectoplasm out there, which is now waiting for us. You see, it can't take a living body, only a dead one, but if its victims agree to come willingly then it will grant them a desire or wish, but if it has to wait until they die then it punishes them by constantly taunting them with glimpses of the life it took from them.'

'Once again, Spud, you have the knack of making my future sound so alluring and reassuring that I can hardly wait,' jokes Monty as his mouth begins to seize up.

'I think it's time you called upon your third eye or inner eye or any eye for that matter to get us out of here before it's too late,' yells Sam.

The ectoplasm moves closer and they see their own reflections staring back at them as it begins to imitate the bodies that it's slowly draining the life force from. But just at the moment the Grim Reaper is about to collect, Charity reaches into her pocket and pulls out one single tarot card that's completely blank on both sides. One side black and the other white, except for a red dot in the middle as she throws it into the air where it stops, dead centre, floating above them.

The card metamorphoses into a pair of magnificent blood-red wings that separate and fly out of the circle, one to the left and one to the right, as they transform into powerful angels. The first becomes the dazzling **Angel**

199

of Judgement with his flowing emerald green and gold robes, golden hair, red wings and horn of judgement. The second is the **Angel of Justice**, resplendent in his silk robes of ruby red and golden crown of justice upon his head. He's seated upon his throne, bearing the scales of justice in his left hand balanced by the sword of justice in his right. He's the Angel of Providence. Truth will out as he seeks justice, while the **Angel of Judgement** passes sentence.

Two mighty angels sent by their Lord to pass judgement and Sentence upon those souls who seek redemption and justice in the **Court of Past Souls**.

The clock of time has come full circle and the **15th August** in the year **2005** is upon them as the court sits for the last time and the fate of not only Polly Melrose, but also Charity will be decided...

The horn of judgement is sounded as the room expands and transforms into a large courtroom encased within the timeless space of the spirit world with the RING no longer trapped within the circle of ectoplasm but seated in the main courtroom. Charity stands alone, looking up at her Lord's mighty messengers, who float high above her with their wings spread wide as they preside over the court. In one corner of the courtroom, imprisoned in a ring of fire, is the evil **spirit of white silk**, while over on the other side of the room is its co-conspirator the **fallacious spirit** in the guise of her charge, the **old woman** alias the **bag lady**, alias Polly Melrose, the **patient**.

Finally, seated in the jury box are the twelve **past souls** whose paths have crossed that of the accused and whose fate now lies in the final judgement of the court. Roland and Vera Uppingham with their twins Harold and Hilary are seated next to their children, Victor and Jean, her husband John and their twins Craig and Alexandra. In the next row are Elsie Pritchard, General Winkner and finally the Captain of the HMS *Emperor*.

The jury: twelve past souls, some who seek vengeance and others forgiveness from the accused, but all of whose fate will be decided by the court on this day the **15th August 2005**.

'Are you ready to present your case, Charity?' commands the **Angel of Judgement** as his voice reverberates around the court.

She looks up at him, her body shaking and her throat dry, as she replies, 'I am.'

'Then let the trial commence,' the angel replies as he blows his horn again.

She turns to face her charge, Polly Melrose, **the fallacious spirit**, who sits in the defendant's pulpit, the epitome of the frail 85-year-old spirit who called to her for help in the hospital ward. Then she looks over at the vile pile of floating ectoplasm imprisoned in the angel's circle of fire, **the spirit of white silk**, who is also Polly Melrose? Which one is the real defendant and which one false?

She walks over to the jury, twelve souls eager to pass sentence, and yet as her **third-eye** looks deep into their inner minds she sees that not all are what they appear to be. Finally she looks out into the courtroom at the RING, where her beloved Monty and the others emanate their love and support, while desperately trying to hide their own inner fears.

Turning back to face the court, she begins her defence.

'I recognise this court as just and true, but there are dark, evil, and fallacious spirits here who seek to deceive and destroy. I will draw them out and eradicate them, sending them back to their master, who seeks only destruction and vengeance and who has no right of place in this court.'

201

The **Angel of Justice** sits up in his throne, still wielding his sword, but resting his scales at his feet before speaking.

'Brave and honest words, Charity, but you were deceived and evil has entered this court, which the purest of inceptors would have seen. You've brought this darkness upon the court and when all is done and sentence is passed upon your charge then you must be brought to account. How do you plead?'

The RING hold their breaths as they wait for her answer.

'Let the defence of my charge be my plea.'

'So be it, Charity,' the angel replies as his words ricochet around the courtroom, bringing with them the feeling of impending doom.

'I look to the jury to begin my defence,' says Charity as she continues. 'Sixty-five years ago a young and innocent girl set out on a journey full of hope and aspiration, but her love and trust was betrayed, which led her into a dark place where she has remained, waiting for redemption. Yes, she did wrong and yes, she has been punished, but what of those who led her into the path of destruction, should they not be punished too? Today they will reap the consequences of their actions and justice will be done.

'Harold and Hilary Uppingham, you deceived and betrayed Polly for money with rancour and greed in your souls and your punishment must be absolute.'

The bitter spirit of Hilary screams, 'But she stole our list and destroyed our future and our children's future.'

'You were the instigators and now you must face the consequences. Guilty as charged, and I ask the court to sentence these souls.'

The **Angel of Judgement** blows his horn as he looks down upon Harold and Hilary to pass judgement. They can't believe that they are being sentenced when they thought that they would be passing judgement.

202

'This court is a mockery and our master will protect us,' shouts Harold.

'There is only one master in this court and he isn't yours. Judgement has been passed and guilty is the verdict,' the angel replies.

With that the **Angel of Justice** picks up his scales and instantly Harold and Hilary find themselves standing within them as they see his sword wielding its way towards them. He strikes through their ghostly bodies and they're sent, screaming, to their fate: the pit of hell; the Dark Life.

Charity moves on. 'Roland and Vera Uppingham, you protected your children with a lie that destroyed another whose innocence was in your charge and now you seek revenge when there would be none to seek if you had told the truth.'

Vera and Roland stand up, violently denying the accusation.

'She lied and deceived us, stealing our son from us with her body when we took her into our home and gave her protection. She deserves her fate and we deserve release from this purgatory.'

The **Angel of Judgement** blows his horn as he passes judgement.

'An innocent soul came into your home and a tainted one left. You and only you are responsible for this as innocence should be protected and not maligned. Guilty as charged.'

Roland and Vera find themselves facing the same fate as their children when the **Angel of Justice** wields his sword again and their souls evaporate from his scales into the dark side of the spirit world, where they're reunited with their children in their eternal misery.

Charity looks upon the remaining Uppingham dynasty. Victor and Jean, aged 55, and John, 60, with their twins

Craig and Alexandra, now 30 years old. What a sight they are, their bodies ravaged and indelibly marked with the ugliness of their lives. Not for them the graceful journey into adulthood and middle age, where the bond of friendship and love grows strong, but the decline into resentful relationships that have left them scared and alone.

There is Victor, who still lives alone and fights the nightmares that come to him in the dead of night with only the paid company of ugly, grasping men to protect him, who've ravaged his body with disease. As the years have passed, the money has dwindled, gone on drugs and endless shallow lovers who've drained him of every ounce of goodness until only a hollow, bitter man remains with poverty as his final companion.

Then there's Jean and John; still together, but whose paths are so steeped in blood and torment that there is no way back into the light for them. They've tortured and killed in the search for false gold, which has still eluded them and now they live in the darkness of their own creation. There is no more money lending business or empire to run as betrayal has become their prison, where the hunter has became the hunted. They hide within the fortress of their dark, bleak house, afraid to venture out unless surrounded by an army of paid bodyguards, who dwindle slowly as the money runs out and the loyalty with it. They've come to the end of the road, where their enemies have grown so vast that they're just waiting for that final knock of death upon the door.

Lastly, there's the final remaining descendants of the crumbling Uppingham Dynasty: Craig and Alexandra, whose lives have descended into the depravity of their own making. Cast out from their own family for their evil mind games that they even performed upon their own parents, they now reside in the place that once gave them such pleasures: The Willows. Rebuilt with modern technology, it has become their impenetrable prison, where they've been sentenced to life in psychiatric care for unspeakable crimes against their fellow man and where they are forced to succumb to horrendous and endless mind tests in the search for the darkness that lurks within their souls.

Five Souls who sit in judgement upon their victim, seeking justice and redemption from their pitiful lives, but who are still unable to see what the truth is as Charity looks to the court for final judgement.

'You sit here today passing judgement upon your victim without regret or remorse and ask this court to pass sentence upon her and release you from your torment. How can you expect mercy when none was given? How can you expect forgiveness when remorse or sorrow is not shown? How can you expect justice when you understand nothing of its purity or truth? Look within yourselves and know that you shall now reap the consequences of your lives.'

The horn sounds again as the **Angel of Judgement** speaks. 'You have entered this court through the doorway of your dreams and when you wake your nightmare will begin. You are guilty as charged and sentence will be passed.'

As they scream, their cries of despair aren't heard, for they are but shadows of themselves in the darkness of their own dreams. When they awake the reality of their crimes will become their fate.

The **Angel of Justice** wields his mighty sword and strikes through them all, sending them back to their fate, which each and every one of them knows will one day end at the gates of hell.

The last three remaining souls, Elsie, the General and Captain await their fate as Charity asks them all the same question, 'What do you three seek from this court?'

205

They all look at Polly, who has watched in silence as all the jurors have been judged and sentenced one by one, as they answer, 'Justice'.

Charity says nothing as the **Angel of Judgement** sounds his horn and they hear that powerful voice again.

'You were spiteful, cowardly and weak, looking to save yourselves through the sacrifice of another, but now seek neither revenge nor redemption. You've paid a heavy price for your sins and justice shall be done.'

As they await their fate, the **Angel of Justice** places them in his scales, but instead of wielding his sword and sending them to darkness, he taps them on their shoulders.

'I release you from your sentence and peace shall now be yours.'

Their bodies float into the air, high above the court, as they look down upon Charity, who smiles up at them as they disappear into the light of the afterlife.

Finally, Charity looks upon her charge, but who and where is the real Polly?

The **fallacious spirit** who sits in the defendant's chair looking frail and innocent or the **spirit of white silk** imprisoned in the circle of fire. Quickly she turns to look at Monty for reassurance as he smiles lovingly back at her, knowing that one mistake now will mean her doom.

She turns to face her Lord's two mighty angels as she pleads her case for Polly. 'Your eminences, there is one soul missing from the jury, but whose path has crossed that of my charge.'

'Where is this soul?' the **Angel of Judgement** asks.

'He's been here all the time, waiting.'

'Reveal him, but know this, if you are wrong and accuse falsely then you shall be judged by this court,' the angel replies.

Anxiously she turns to face the **spirit of white silk**.

'I know who you really are and call you out. It's time to reveal your true self.'

The court is silent as the ectoplasm imprisoned within the circle of fire remains still and quiet, just as it's been all through the proceedings.

'You must reveal yourself otherwise I win and you lose,' Charity commands, taunting it.

Slowly a silhouette forms within the circle of fire until eventually the frail and emaciated body of 85-year-old Mr Parr walks free and into the centre of the courtroom, which sends a shiver down the spine of Aunt Lizzy, who was only talking to him the other day when he was still very much alive.

The two angels look to each other and wonder who this frail old man really is as he walks through their impenetrable circle of fire.

'At last I see you,' says Charity as she desperately tries to hide the fear within her voice.

'What do you see, Charity? Do you see my right of passage over your soul?' he says in that frail, yet somehow menacing voice of his.

She doesn't reply as she turns to face the court and reveals the final chapter in the life of Polly Melrose.

'Polly didn't die in 2005 aged eighty-five but on **15th August 1965** at only forty-five, when she made a pact with the dark side to save her from her torturer, Harold, who was sent by his master, Lucifer, to torment her thoughts until her mind broke and she could bear it no longer. That same day he sent Mr Parr, who had long since been his servant; he uncovered some discrepancies in Harold's accounts at the Bank of England, where he had been posted on temporary secondment. Remembering what Harold's father had asked him to do back in 1940 and curious to discover the outcome, he laboriously checked the records at the Bank of Canada and Sun Life building when he came across Harold's six bogus accounts and the stolen two million. But how was he to get to the money without the other corresponding accounts? He racked his brains without success until late one night, on **15th August 1945**, there was a knock on the door and Lucifer entered in the form of the Enchanter, offering him the answer, Harold's missing list, and all he had to do was sell his soul.

'With the two million in his possession the good life began for Mr Parr until twenty years later on the **15th August 1965** Lucifer called again to claim his soul, but offered him a reprieve. All he had to do was get Polly to trade her soul for peace of mind, which she did when their paths crossed at the hospital and where Lucifer stole her essence in the form of the **spirit of white silk**, leaving her shell of a body behind, damned forever. But Lucifer was tempted to taste the pleasures of living flesh and so, through the demon entity of ectoplasm, entered the body of the ward sister, who took Polly's identity and briefly claimed her benefit before she too was driven into the pit of madness as she inherited Polly's dark thoughts.

'How delicious it must have been for Lucifer to watch the Uppinghams torture the woman that they thought was Polly, knowing that they would never learn her secret because her body was indeed "blank". How could she feel pain when she didn't exist, except in the illusion of ectoplasm as Lucifer played his evil games on everyone?

'It was 1987 when Polly's corpse disappeared, death number two, but how could she die when she didn't really exist? The **spirit of white silk** never dies, it moves from one body to the next as it entered the lifeless body of a **bag lady** that lay dying in the filth of the streets outside the hospital. The third and final chapter in the life of Polly Melrose.'

Charity stops and looks over at Polly, when for a moment

she weakens, as she knows that once she calls him out there's no going back.

'You win, and I lose.'

The courtroom is still as all eyes are upon Polly who sits there, still and cold, as she looks over at Mr Parr, who melts into a pile of silky white liquid that travels along the floor until it reaches her feet, where she's devoured and white becomes black, as two evil spirits become one: the **fallacious** and the **spirit of white silk**; two dark demons that are born out of one, their master, Lucifer.

Out of the black ascends the darkest demon of all, the **Devil**, the Horned Goat of Mendes and Charity's arch enemy.

'At last your quest has ended, Charity, and now you can save your precious charge, Polly, who waits for her name to be placed upon her gravestone and be released from her torment.'

The two angels spread their wings as they prepare for battle.

'You dare to enter this court, knowing that you cannot win against our Lord,' commands the **Angel of Justice** as he wields his mighty sword, while the **Angel of Judgement** prepares to destroy his enemy by calling upon the heavens with his horn.

Lucifer spreads his great bat wings, imprisoning Charity, as the courtroom turns to darkness and the fires of hell surround them. Monty and the others watch, powerless to save her.

'Call upon your mighty Lord, but before he comes she will be mine.'

'What is it that you really want, if she's already yours?' the angels ask, knowing that they can destroy him, but not before he sends her to her fate.

'I will release Polly if Charity will renounce her powers

as an inceptor and come with me willingly, as did her sister Annie.'

Those words cut through Charity like a steel sword for she was always told that her beloved sister died of an illness that was hereditary, the same one that took her mother, but no one, not even Aunt Lizzy, would ever tell her what that illness was.

Those dark thoughts return again, but this time with a vengeance. What dark seed is within her that torments her so? Has it always been there, lying dormant, waiting to be released? And what of her sister Annie? Why does she never visit her from the spirit world or come to her in her psychic dreams offering comfort and love like her beloved parents, and why do they never mention her name?

What is she to do? She knows that while under his wings his dark powers are stronger than hers and that help will come too late to save her; she's already damned...

If she renounces her powers as an inceptor then she betrays her Lord and all that she is. But if she doesn't then she betrays her word to Polly, which is sacrosanct to an inceptor, when she promised to give her back her name.

Which is the greater betrayal?

Whatever decision she makes, she will have to face the consequences of that choice.

Which one will it be?